I0744379

VIRGO

ZODIAC HEAT
BOOK ONE

MIA LONDON

Virgo

by Mia London

This is a work of fiction. Names, characters, places and incidents either are the product of the author's imagination or are used factitiously, and any resemblance to actual persons, living or dead, business establishments, event or locales is entirely coincidental.

Copyright ©2023 Mia London Books

All rights reserved. No part of this book may be reproduced or utilized in any form or by any means, electronic or mechanical, including photocopying, recording, or by any information storage and retrieval system, without permission from the publisher.

ISBN 978-1955369152 (ebook)

ISBN 978-1955369169 (paperback)

Publisher: Mia London Books

PO Box 93852

Southlake, TX 76092

Cover By: Renee Luke

Interior Design: Creative As Hale Designs

Chapter One

Home. It was always good to be home—comforting and welcoming—the time for homecooked food instead of rushed crap at the apartment or a drive-thru.

Isabella Walker stepped out of her car, and, before shutting the door, she breathed in a lungful of air. Like somehow, the air at home was better than at Emerald. She didn't have the energy to lug her stuff inside, but she had to. She made several trips, dropped the overstuffed laundry bag by the washer, then dragged her luggage upstairs to her childhood bedroom.

Finals were done. Hallelujah!

Her junior year at Emerald University was in the bag.

Normally, she would have stayed back with her friends and got her party on for the weekend. But Chloe's parents had planned a family cruise, and she wanted to get home to get everything packed since they'd be gone for five days. And Brianne thought she was coming down with the flu and had driven home the night before.

Just as well, Iz was spent. Her finals went well overall.

She'd studied her ass off and survived on Ramen, takeout, and lots of coffee.

Now, she had the summer to herself. She could reconnect with her girls in a few weeks. Her parent's house was only a two-hour drive from Emerald, but Chloe lived just an hour south of the house, and Brianne was an hour west. Maybe she could have them over for Memorial Day weekend. They could hang by the pool and drink some of Reed's delicious rum punches.

Oh, yes! Brilliant.

For now, she needed a shower—a nice, long hot shower. Then some food followed by hibernation. Well, at least a two-hour nap before dinner. *Maybe Mom will make meatloaf.*

Iz put away most of her clothes and plopped her toiletries on the vanity.

The house was quiet, as to be expected. Mom would be at the real estate office or showing houses. She tried not to office out of the home, she'd said it distracted her. And Reed, her stepdad would, for sure, be at his office downtown. He was an attorney, in-house counsel with GS&M.

She stripped and turned the shower faucet on full. Dipping her head under the hot spray, she felt nothing could compare to being home. Her own bathroom, her own bed, no nosy neighbors or partiers coming in at three in the morning.

After several long minutes, Iz stepped out and wrapped a towel around herself. Her stomach growled. She needed sustenance.

She padded down the stairs to the kitchen and fished through the fridge for something that'd pass for lunch. Well, it wasn't as stocked as usual. The past few years, her mom had loaded the kitchen with ready-to-eat food and leftovers for Izzy's summer and holiday breaks from school. Of course, Iz was home earlier than expected. They probably weren't expecting her until Sunday afternoon.

She lifted the tinfoil from a bowl seeing goulash. Perfect. She set it in the microwave oven, hit start, then retrieved a glass from the cabinet.

She heard a noise.

What was that?

She froze. She thought she might have imagined it, except there it was again.

Shit! Someone was in the office.

Her little heart pounded in her chest. She scanned the countertops; her cell phone was upstairs. She quietly lifted a butcher knife out of the wooden block and stopped the microwave.

Did she forget to lock the front door behind her? This was a safe neighborhood, but one could never know for sure.

Clutching her bath towel and the other hand gripping the knife, she made slow steps toward the office.

The office chair creaked.

She swallowed hard and turned the corner, knife thrust straight in front of her. She turned the door handle, lunged through the doorway, and yelled. "Hey!"

Reed spun around in his chair, eyes wide. "Iz?"

Isabella lowered her arm. Her entire chest heaved as she tried to catch her breath.

"Reed? What are you doing here?"

The corner of his lip lifted. "I could ask you the same thing."

She crossed the hardwood floors and set the knife on the edge of his desk. "Finals are done, so I came back early. I'll see Chloe and Brianne later. Why are you home early from work?"

He rose and placed his hands on her bare shoulders as he kissed her cheek. "I had some stuff to do, so I took off work early. I didn't hear you."

He'd looked like he'd been staring out the window.

"I suppose you haven't spoken to your mother lately."

Iz tipped her head. "No. Why?"

He pursed his lips, took a breath, and began. "I figured. Iz, there's no good way to say this so I'm just going to come right out with it. Your mother and I are getting a divorce."

Her mouth fell open. "What?" Her voice was as quiet as a church mouse. She heard the words, but she couldn't believe it.

He looked down at her. "Why don't you get dressed, and we can talk in the kitchen."

"No, please, tell me now. I thought you two were happy."

Reed was the best thing to happen to their family. When her mom married Reed, her life had made a one-eighty. Iz had been busted for skipping school, cheating, getting into fights on the playground. After Reed, she got into competitive volleyball and won a partial academic scholarship to Emerald, which was notoriously challenging to get into. Reed came in and was like a stabilizing force in her life. Even her mom seemed less manic.

Thinking about her family being broken up ripped her heart into pieces.

Reed rested a hip against the desk and sighed. "It's not pretty. I suspected she'd been cheating for a while, but I denied it. I confronted her last week, and she admitted it. Some thirty-year-old newbie realtor in the office." He flapped a hand in the air like it was inconsequential. And it was. The *who* didn't matter. All that mattered was the fact that Miranda'd cheated.

Her mother was always so self-centered. She valued people who could do something for her. The world revolved around her. She was first; everyone else was second.

Iz had come to accept it, of course, but as Miranda's one-and-only child, she hadn't experienced the *peculiarities* of her mother's character like others had.

That explained why Reed looked so tired. He was still a

handsome man, broad shoulders, handsome face, and expressive chocolate eyes.

Reed trained his eyes on her, and after a moment of processing, the tears pricked the backs of her eyes. She had family...that was breaking up. Her stability, her rock, suddenly a house of cards ready to tumble.

"Oh, gees, Iz, c'mere." He opened his arms, and she stepped in. He wrapped her in a cocoon of warmth and caring, and she dared to wonder how long she'd get to keep that.

The flood gates opened, and she sobbed into his shoulder.

He held her tighter, and her arms looped around his neck. She didn't want to lose him. Whenever her mother was acting crazy, Reed had always been a grounding force, talking sense into her and ultimately making her relationship with her mother better.

But that wasn't the worst of it. The thought of missing him killed her. She might never see him again and she loved him. He was more of a father to her than her *own* father.

The crying didn't cease. Iz tried to pull herself together, but she could only think about Reed not being a part of her life.

Finally, she spoke. "Reed, I'm scared of what my life looks like without you."

He pulled her away to meet her gaze, his eyes slightly glassy. "Without me?"

She shrugged a shoulder. "What's the chance I'll see you anymore after the divorce is finalized?"

"No, precious. I'm not going anywhere. I may not have adopted you, but make no mistake, you are mine." His voice became firmer as he spoke. "I'm keeping the house, and this is your home too. You live here whenever you want, during college breaks. Hell, even after college."

"Really?" The tears slowly dried up.

"Really. Your mother wants one of those new condos downtown. I'm keeping the house. I love this house."

"I do too."

He brushed away the last of her tears from her cheeks.

She pecked his lips and returned to their fierce hug. "God, I thought that was it. That after this summer, I'd never see you again."

He shook his head. "I'll share you during the holidays, if that's what I have to do, but I'm not going anywhere."

A small smile pulled at her lips. She pecked his lips again. "I'm so glad. I'm sorry about Mom, though. She was different with you, and I thought you were her happily-ever-after."

He smirked.

There was nothing more to be said. Reed was resilient, and he still had her, even if she'd spend most of her time two hours away.

She cupped his cheeks and kissed his lips again, this time lingering longer, and she didn't know why. She nearly gasped. Quickly, she regained composure and smiled big. "Well, Mom's mistake because you really are a wonderful man. Now, I have to go eat something, I'm starved. Want anything?"

He paused, then returned the smile. "I'm good. I need to get some documents together for the attorney. Let's have dinner around seven, okay?"

"Great." She pivoted to make her way to the kitchen.

She let out a shaky breath. *Holy crap! What was that?*

She'd strung out that last kiss for some unknown reason. Maybe it was like a release of emotion because he would still be in her life. Maybe it was just plain brain fog and exhaustion from finals.

But how was it that she loved it so much? She was out of her mind.

Reed was her stepdad, a father figure. He taught her how to drive, how to jumpstart her car battery, and, ironically, how to dance. She admired him. The only emotion between them was familial, not romantic.

She quickly grabbed her goulash and water and high-tailed it to her bedroom to get dressed. She was a smart woman. There was likely a perfectly fine explanation for what had just happened, like a hormone spike or sympathy over his breakup with Mom.

Best thing she could do was to put this behind her. She had the summer to relax, find a part-time job and bank some cash, and hang with her friends. She didn't have a boyfriend, but that was a possibility too.

It was all Reed could do to concentrate on making chili.

Iz was torn up about the divorce and, it turned out, scared of losing him. That would never happen. But then she kissed him. Although it was a closed-mouth kiss, and certainly not their first one, this one had been different.

Fuck! It sent some kind of damn lust racing through him in that instant, and that didn't make any damn sense. She was his daughter, for all intents.

He was pretty sure she hadn't thought anything of it, but he'd replayed it a thousand times and needed to get it out of his head. She *could not* be on his mind in that way. Sure, she was smart, kind, and had grown into a beautiful woman, but the age difference alone...

No, don't even justify not being with her because you're not gonna be with her.

Reed knew deep inside it was a fluke, probably long forgotten by the next day. He served the chili when he heard Iz's footfalls down the stairs. A smile firmly pasted on his face because she was the apple of his eye, and they should enjoy their summer together since they might not have very many more together. Exactly.

CHAPTER TWO

Reed woke up hard. *What the fuck!*

He hadn't done that in years. Sex with Miranda had been good, but it had trickled down the last few years. So, his johnson had been able to keep his cool, knowing no satisfaction would be coming soon.

Now seemed to be a different story. His cock had the impression that fun was on the horizon.

Again, what the fuck?

It was Saturday. He couldn't go to the office to avoid her. That would be obvious--time to work on the outdoor projects that had been piling up.

He threw on an old T-shirt and shorts and made his way to find coffee. He passed Iz's door to see it closed. She'd likely sleep until noon. Dinner the prior night had gone without incident, and the conversation flowed as it always had, to his relief.

Reed wrote out a list over his egg breakfast of things to accomplish.

Clean out gutters

Mulch front flower beds/back beds
Scrub mildew off back pavers
Power wash windows
Organize garage

The last one would take an entire day. So, if thoughts of Iz didn't subside after today, he'd have a project for Sunday.

First up, a trip to Home Depot for mulch.

Isabella woke up refreshed and...horny. She might need to make finding a boyfriend a priority because thoughts of Reed were wreaking havoc on her nerves...and her pussy.

Dammit!

And to top it off, she had to call her mother today.

After she donned a bikini and grabbed a towel from the closet, she headed to the kitchen. There was no sign of Reed, but that was probably a good thing.

Dinner the previous night seemed to go fine, so she knew all of this was in her head, and she could cast it away just as quickly as it had come. Although, in all honesty, she'd always had a thing for mature, confident men, not necessarily older men. Truthfully, Reed was all that and downright handsome as sin. He'd likely have a girlfriend before the summer was out. Good for him.

Movement caught her eye outside. Reed was scattering mulch in the flowerbeds by the pool patio. It looked nice. He looked nice. His shirt was off, and the sweat glistened off his back muscles. She swallowed. His physique was incredible for a forty-six-year-old man.

Turn away, she scolded herself.

After a late breakfast/early lunch, Iz put in a load of laundry, then grabbed her sunglasses, phone, and suntan lotion.

She could handle a fair amount of sun, and her skin turned a golden brown which she loved. And after months of being cooped up in classrooms and her apartment, it felt great to finally embrace the Texas summer.

She dropped her towel on the chaise with her other things and strode toward Reed.

"Hey."

"Hi." He looked up briefly. "I didn't hear you."

"This looks nice." She looked from the beds to him.

"Thanks." He rose to stretch out his back, surveying the progress.

"So, do we have any plans next weekend, Memorial Day weekend?"

He paused a moment. "Not that I know of."

"Do you mind if I have a few friends over one night? Maybe even have Chloe and Brianne spend a night or two?"

"No, I don't mind."

"Great. Thanks." She smiled and felt the compulsion to peck his lips again but quickly stepped back and made her way back to the recliner.

She had no idea what was coming over her, but nothing that a conversation with her mother couldn't squash.

"Izzy, honey. How are you?"

"Hi, Mom. I'm home."

"Home?" Her voice rose an octave. "I wasn't expecting you until tomorrow."

"I know. I talked to Reed."

"Ah, so he told you?"

"Yeah. What's going on?"

"Oh, Iz, sometimes marriages don't work out."

This is husband number two. Her first husband, Iz's father, hadn't been the brightest candle in the menorah. But Reed? Reed was the best, and Miranda had blown it.

"Reed and I gave it a try but decided parting would be the best."

How hard did you try in another man's bed?

Her mother yammered on about her new place, her job, and anything else centered on her. Until finally... "So enough about me. How did school go? What are your plans for the summer?"

Get laid.

Oops! Best not to say that out loud. "Visit friends and get a job. Nothing big."

"No summer classes?"

"No, not this year. I'm right on schedule for graduation, according to my advisor. Plus, I'll get credit for the internship with the Environmental Challenge Group." She always had to say the full name of the company she'd work for. Saying ECG would only get her blank stares.

"Okay, great, honey. Well, I have houses to show this weekend, but let's get together next week."

"Okay, Mom."

Her mom told her she loved her and disconnected the line. Iz believed the words, but she was pretty sure Miranda loved herself more than she loved her.

She chuckled lightly because Miranda would never change, and Iz knew never expect her to.

After some time, she flipped onto her stomach and recoated suntan lotion. Then to minimize her tan lines, she pulled loose the string of her bikini top and laid flat against her chest to text her friends.

A few text exchanges and her girls were in for Memorial Day. Plus, they both could come Friday to hang. Iz sent a shout-out to a few other friends for next Saturday night, too. Maybe Reed could do his delicious burgers on the grill.

Speaking of Reed, where was he?

She scanned over her sunglasses to see him still working in

the flower beds. She wondered what got him so motivated. Maybe without Mom around, he could do what he wanted to the property.

Iz placed her hands under her face and closed her eyes until she heard her phone chime with texts about the party Saturday.

Reed couldn't miss Iz suntanning beside the pool. He was out here working to forget about her for a while. Of course, seeing her in that blue bikini didn't help. Not one damn bit.

He had no idea what had gotten into him when it came to Iz. Perhaps he should think about setting up a date soon and get his mind back onto someone in his own age bracket.

What was the acceptable mourning timeframe for a seven-year marriage?

An hour had passed, and the mulching was done. He was thirsty, starving, and hot. He slipped off his shoes and socks, made sure there was nothing in his pockets, and dove into the pool.

Iz hadn't moved in a while. She might have fallen asleep.

He stepped out of the pool and reached for a towel. He strode over to her and heard her steady, even breathing. She faced the other way, but leaning over, he could see her eyes were closed. He hated to bother her, but he didn't want her to burn either.

"Iz." He called quietly. "Iz." He gently rocked her with his hand on her shoulder.

"What?" She bolted up onto her elbows and turned, squinting in the light to look at him.

Shit! Her top wasn't covering her chest in this position. He had a clear view of the side of her naked breasts.

"Um, sorry. You'd fallen asleep, and I didn't want you to burn."

She blinked more, still in a sleepy state, and adjusted her sunglasses. "Oh, okay. Thanks." She lay back down and reached for the lotion bottle.

He quickly spun around and headed for the house. Yeah, the entire To-Do list was getting done this weekend. That sneak peek might have just set him back a week.

After a long day of outdoor labor, Reed had successfully worked himself into exhaustion. Iz had come outside late in the afternoon while he was working on the gutters to see if she could make dinner for them.

Absolutely.

By seven that night, he'd strolled downstairs, the smell of chicken fajitas in the air. He'd taken a tepid shower—the warmth from the sun radiating from his skin—and put on fresh clothes. He might just collapse into bed early that night.

Iz heard him and stopped her chopping to pull out the water pitcher from the fridge and a bottle of beer from the freezer.

Dang! She knew what he liked—extra cold beer after a long day outside.

"Thanks." He filled a tall glass with cold water. He chugged the entire thing.

"You're welcome." She smiled up at him as she returned to her task. "Talked to Mom today."

"Oh." He took a seat at the island, watching her work on their dinner.

"She was typical Mom, lots of talking about herself."

"Ah, yes."

Iz paused and looked at him. "It's funny. It's sorta calmer around here without her." She scooped the tomatoes into a bowl with the other ingredients for pico de gallo. "Anyway, we're supposed to get together this week."

"Okay, good. What can I do?"

"Uh, maybe just put everything on the table. It's basically ready."

They sat, and he dug in. He was famished, and Iz made good fajitas.

"So, what are your plans for the summer?"

"Well, I'll apply to a few jobs. I can do that online. But outside of the party Saturday—"

"A party?"

She paused mid-bite. "A small gathering."

"How many people are we talkin', Iz?"

"No more than twenty."

He held back his shock. He would give her anything, really. He just wasn't sure he could throw a party for twenty without Miranda here. He took a breath. "Okay." He urged her to continue.

"Well, outside of that, I think I'll take a few road trips."

This had him curious. "Road trips?"

"Yeah. There's a new state-of-the-art recycling facility going in in southwest Houston I'd like to see. And I think I can get in some aquifer investigation outside of Austin."

He was so proud of Izzy. She was working on her a degree in Environmental Science, and truly believed with enough of the right changes, we could create a healthier planet and a more sustainable way of living. "Okay, well, I have some time off, so if you want someone to ride along with you or share the driving, I'll go."

Her eyebrows lifted. "You will?"

"Sure."

She beamed. "Thanks, Reed. That'd be great. I'll keep you posted."

Dinner finished, and Iz had been right. The place did seem calmer without Miranda around.

A wash of guilt came over him. Shouldn't he feel more

sorrow about his marriage ending? Shouldn't he have more tears, a loss of appetite, and all that?

"Let's watch a movie tonight," she spoke, breaking his train of thought over his soon-to-be ex-wife.

"Sounds good."

Reed stacked the dishwasher as Iz wiped down the counters and put away the few dinner leftovers. They cleaned up in relative silence. If Reed was affected by the incident earlier by the pool, he had a great way of hiding it.

Iz hadn't exactly dozed off, more like daydreaming. It was crazy how Reed had filled her thoughts lately. Occasionally, her friends had made comments about how good-looking Reed was, but she never gave it much thought. Of course, she could see he was attractive; many women had thought so. But she was his stepdaughter. Now, the thoughts were front and center that this attractive man would no longer be her stepfather. And Iz couldn't help wanting to catch his attention.

When Reed had come over to wake her up, a spontaneous thought popped in her head. An idea to flash him her boobs. She hoped to get his attention, maybe have him start thinking of her as something other than a daughter figure. Because truly, they had become friends over the past few years, and his role as a father had diminished. She knew he respected and admired her, and Iz, at least, wanted to try to capitalize on that and see if they could have more. It was risky —changing the relationship into a romantic one—but the more she thought about it, the more she knew she had to try. She'd kick herself if she didn't at least try, but Reed didn't seem to take much notice of her, so she'd have to test the waters.

After the movie, she rose. "Okay, I need to head upstairs. I have loads of laundry waiting for me to fold. Good night."

"G'night, Iz." He briefly glanced her way, then back to the TV.

Hmm.

He rarely did that. He would always make *full* eye contact with her. Maybe he wasn't *completely* unaffected.

She smiled to herself.

Iz headed to the shower, and within twenty minutes, she was clean and smooth. She slathered on the lotion to help her tan last longer, blotted her long, wet hair, and wrapped the bath towel around herself. Next stop, in search of Reed.

CHAPTER THREE

R eed turned off the TV and headed to his office. Although it was only Saturday, he liked to plan his week. It helped him feel ready for the next day and kept him on track to accomplish what he needed to. As in-house counsel for GS&M Incorporated, every contract—incoming or outbound—went through his department. He prepared and audited the company's legal reports and drafted the language for anything with a legal ramification from the CEO's response to a scandal to the privacy policy on their website.

A patent infringement case brought to him by a member of his team was the shark closest to the boat. It seemed a company in Taiwan thought they could copy some of GS&M's patented chip technology without permission.

Ha, he chuckled to himself. No one who wanted to steal technology would ever ask.

He'd been working just fifteen minutes when Iz strolled in, fresh from her shower.

"Hey."

"Hey." She smiled and made her way to his place behind

the desk. "I saw that you washed my car today. Got all the bugs off. I forgot to say thank you, so I wanted to come do that now."

"Oh, you're welcome."

She leaned, and with a hand on his shoulder, pressed a kiss to his lips. Her lips were soft and warm. It felt very much like the one from the day before, except maybe longer.

She then rose, smiled again, and made her way toward the door. As she walked, she loosened her towel, swung it to the side and grabbed her long hair to blot the water. She was completely nude, although he only had sight to her backside, her heart-shaped ass slowly sauntering away.

His cock came instantly alive.

"Iz," he growled out low in warning.

She knew what she was doing, little vixen. Earlier, by the pool, when she was half-asleep, he hadn't been sure. Now? Now, he was a hundred percent sure. She was stirring up trouble.

She tilted her head back to meet his gaze. "Good night." And she was out the door.

Sonuvabitch! That body on her was amazing—curves in all the right places, tanned and glowing skin, the total package that made a man weak in the knees.

Something happened. Something had changed. Maybe it was yesterday when they spoke, and she told him she was afraid of him leaving her. He'd felt it but couldn't be sure.

Sex hadn't been a priority in the recent past with Miranda. And, of course, now he understood why. She was getting it from someone else.

He could forget a slip once or twice. An accident. But this wasn't an accident. This was a full-blown relationship. A relationship she was supposed to be having with *him*, not some boy toy from work. Reed knew Miranda wouldn't change, couldn't change, so he was out.

He figured a pent-up supply of testosterone was to blame. *But fuck!* Iz had felt what he felt.

But how...how did he turn her down gently? How did he calm his hormones enough to *not* think about her, dream about her, and want her in the way she seems to now want him?

A relationship was simply out of the question. It couldn't be done. They could *not* get involved romantically. She might be everything a man could dream of, but this man needed to dream about something else. His twenty-year-old soon-to-be ex-stepdaughter was off limits. Period.

Holy crap, that felt good. Iz knew she was playing with fire, taunting Reed like that, but she wanted him. And now, he knew it too. Beyond a shadow of a doubt. The ball was in his court.

She heard the caution in his voice when he'd called her name, but she knew him. There was *no* bite to it. If he really wanted to shut it down, he would have. An attorney and a Virgo, he was Mr. Fix-It. If her playful flirting was unwanted, he would have told her under no uncertain terms could they have any romantic involvement.

God! She nearly beamed inside with triumph.

She wanted Reed so badly, if he'd called her back, she would have gone. She would have dropped the towel for his hands and lips to have free reign of her body. If he wanted her on his desk, she would have given herself to him.

Shit! Just the thought was making her wet.

She wanted Reed. She had to have him. Now, she'd exercise some patience to see what he'd do, but she had time. She had a little Memorial Day party to plan for. Then, the entire summer was theirs.

CHAPTER FOUR

Sunday morning, Reed awoke again with a boner. This was getting ridiculous.

You have yourself to blame.

It was true. He should have pulled back when she kissed him yesterday in the office. He'd been kicking himself ever since. Then, she flashed her naked backside to him.

Motherfucker!

His cock sprung to life like a homing beacon.

He'd better find a way to tame this little filly before it got much more out of control. She was hands-off.

Shit! He was starting to sound like a broken record.

Donning some old work clothes, he headed to the garage after breakfast for a long day of hard, sweaty labor, in a place he'd likely not see Izzy and that incredibly sexy body of hers.

Until he could formulate a plan to talk to her without hurting her feelings, he had to avoid her.

Reed was avoiding her. Iz knew it. Rarely did he work this damn much over the weekend, especially when the temperature was supposed to hit ninety. He might do a little chore here and there, but then settle back for a leisurely lunch. Maybe go shopping with Mom. Maybe watch sports on TV or hit the gym.

That's okay, she promised herself. It was actually a good sign that he was avoiding her *and* avoiding talking to her. And why? Probably because he didn't want to tell her No. He wanted what she had to offer. Well, at least that was what Iz prayed for.

After a late breakfast, with no sign of Reed, she went to the garage in search of him.

"Hey."

"Hey." He wiped his brow before lifting a box out of the way.

"I was thinking I'd take out chicken. If you could grill it, I'll do the cold chicken pasta salad for dinner."

He met her gaze and nodded. "Yeah, sounds good."

"Great. Do you need any help?"

The corner of his lip lifted. "Nah, I'm good."

"Okay, I'm gonna run over to the mall in a bit, do a little shopping."

"Okay, have fun."

She spun around and closed the door behind her.

Mall? Ha! She couldn't name one person who went to the mall. No, what she had in mind was not sold in any mall she knew of.

After slipping on her sundress and sandals, then winding her hair into a loose bun, she went downstairs to the kitchen. She filled a tall glass of cold water for Reed and grabbed her purse and car keys.

"Hey"

He looked up at her.

She walked to him and handed him the tall plastic cup. "Thought you might need some."

He smiled back at her and gulped down half the contents.

She then waved her goodbye and strode to her car. There. That was all pretty harmless. Maybe he'd stop hiding long enough to come inside and chat with her. They actually once enjoyed talking together. And as much as she wanted to get naked with Reed, she also wanted the friendship to stay intact. Was she asking too much?

The thought of losing that friendship made her heart hurt a little.

After a short twenty-minute drive, she'd arrived at her destination, The Velvet Box. The greatest place for adult toys, clothes, and accessories. Iz's quest: a new bikini. Not just any bikini. An eye-popping teeny tiny one. One that would get Reed's attention.

Her current bikinis were all very pretty, maybe even a little sexy. But what she had in mind was something that she'd *never* wear in public.

A smiley redhead greeted her as she crossed the spacious store. "Let me know if you need help finding anything."

"Thanks." Iz took it all in—the sexy lingerie, the masks, the whips, and a wall of various toys. There were scented lotions, lickable lotions, and edible panties. She glanced at the various vibes. Her two vibrators were already fantastic. She really didn't need anything else.

Then, she came upon the first rack of swimsuits. *Oh, yes. This is perfect.*

There were multicolored ones, mesh ones, and one-piece suits with cut-out sides. She lifted an unlined crochet bikini. That would turn his head. *Maybe that's a little too over the top.*

She selected a solid white one and a polka dot one in her size. She went to the dressing room and closed the curtain.

She stripped and started with the white one. The label read "Micro Mini" and was simply gorgeous. The front of the bottoms was a rectangular strip of fabric that just covered her mound in the most minimal way. Thankfully, she'd recently had a Brazilian wax because this suit would not look good with any hair visible.

She turned to look at the back. The back of the bottoms had just a little triangle placed at the top of her crack. She played with the triangle top, and each side could slide for personal taste.

Wow! She loved it. She didn't need to try on the other one. The "virginal white" was perfect for her Virgo man.

CHAPTER FIVE

Tuesday morning, Iz's phone chimed with a text. She was half-asleep, but she could read: Mom.

Hi baby! Can you do lunch today? Meet me at McNamara's. It's close to my new condo and I can show you!

Iz sighed. She typed out a response that she could. She had three interviews lined up that week but nothing for Tuesday. It was probably the best day to meet with her mom.

At noon, Iz sat at a table in McNamara's restaurant, waiting for her "fashionably late" mother to arrive. McNamara's was one of those restaurants where one went to be seen. Iz wasn't surprised that her mom selected it.

And speak of the devil. Fifteen minutes late, her mother glided across the expanse of the restaurant, stopping twice to chat with people Iz didn't recognize. Mom was always on. Well, that's not entirely true. At home, Iz had often seen the real Miranda. She was sometimes crazed with work stuff or some event planning; other times relaxed and appeared to be comfortable in her own skin. The pendulum for her mother swung wildly. Iz, somedays, could hardly keep up.

That said, she still loved her mother and believed she was good inside and meant no harm.

Iz stood.

"Darling, look at you." Miranda hugged her tightly. The Chanel fragrance Iz had come to associate with her mother filled her nostrils.

"Hi, Mom." She smiled back at her mom.

The waiter quickly attended to them, smiling broadly at her mother. Even men decades younger than her mother gravitated toward her. Miranda had a charm and charisma that age surpassed. Anyone who really knew Miranda could see how she ended up in the arms of someone twelve or fourteen years her junior. Iz just thought Miranda had a stronger constitution to turn down any offers.

Poor Reed.

Well, maybe not so poor. Suddenly, a world of possibilities had opened up for him...and Iz.

"So, tell me, darling, how are you? You're glowing. You must be spending time by the pool."

"Some."

"I always loved that pool. So tranquil and relaxing. I can't wait to show you my new place. They have a rooftop pool with a view of downtown."

And that might be a record. Three sentences before Miranda made it about herself.

Iz hid her smile behind her iced tea glass.

Miranda chattered on about so many things and yet managed to ask about Iz. Listening to her mom was entertainment in and of itself. The time flew. Finally, she asked about Reed.

"How is he?" Sincere caring showed in her hazel eyes.

"I think he'll be all right. He seems distracted sometimes, like he's still processing."

Miranda nodded.

Iz wanted to ask how she could cheat on him, but it didn't matter. Really, that was something Miranda would have to live with. And frankly, the next man would likely be on high alert to those tendencies.

"Reed's a good man. So much better than your father. He'll find someone new; I don't doubt it."

Sure, once his heart repairs.

"Someone who can handle the same thing every day." She stuck a bite of cucumber in her mouth.

Iz looked up from her chicken cacciatore. "What?"

"Well, you'll see when you get married. Sometimes marriage can get monotonous."

She's talking about sex.

"I personally need a bit more excitement." She loaded her fork with more salad greens.

Apparently. But couldn't you do something to create that excitement...with your husband?

Frankly, Iz liked excitement too, but she knew how to create it without hurting anyone. That was yet another difference between her and her mom.

After her mom paid the bill, they took the short drive to her high-rise condominium. Everything was new, modern, and shiny—so representative of the next chapter Miranda wanted to create for herself.

Her place was furnished to be shown in home décor magazines around the world: high-end furniture, open-concept floor plan with high ceilings, and modern accents. And yes, a million-dollar view.

"Wow. This is nice, Mom." Iz walked around.

Miranda smiled with pride. "Thanks. I love it. And look," she strode into the kitchen, "I finally got one of those fancy cappuccino machines."

Iz nodded. She had no idea her mother ever wanted one.

Floor-to-ceiling windows were also in the bedroom.

"And look," Iz followed Miranda into a second bedroom that was set up as an office. Double monitors and paper covered the modern glass-top desk. "I finally have an office in my home." She beamed.

Wait. What?

Iz thought Miranda never wanted an office in the home because it was distracting.

Whatever.

Her mom rested a hand on her shoulder. "So, if I don't ask you to stay here, you'll know why. I hope you understand." Miranda gave a sympathetic smile.

"Of course." Iz knew she couldn't stay with her mother anyway. Her mother would make her nuts, and now she could see, her place was with Reed. He needed her, and on some profound level, she needed him. Probably always would.

New place, new furniture, just about everything was new, save for two or three photos of herself and Miranda, there was very little that indicated Miranda had a life in suburbia with a family that had loved her.

Maybe this is what she needs, Izzy thought.

They chatted more before she hugged her mom and left. A melancholy feeling fell over Iz when she thought about her mother's "new life."

Then an image of Reed popped in her head, and a smile pulled at her lips unbidden.

This new chapter in all their lives could be filled with so much hope and...desire. Iz had to admit it—a desire had bubbled up from a place deep inside.

She had an incredibly full life with a bright future, even if she didn't have a boyfriend currently. But now, with this new awareness, she simply couldn't ignore it. She wanted Reed. She had to have him.

Reed's alarm woke him a little earlier than usual. It probably wasn't necessary, but he couldn't risk running into Iz. He even left her a note to order take-out for dinner and that he would have already eaten. He'd likely ask Nitia to have something brought up for the steakhouse three blocks over.

He stripped and stepped under the shower's hot spray coating his body and pummeling his erection. The fifth morning in a row, he'd woken up in this condition. A few jerks gave him temporary relief so he could focus on getting ready.

Thirty minutes later, gym bag in hand, he made his way to the kitchen. He brewed coffee and scrambled three eggs quickly before making his way into the morning rush-hour traffic.

As much as he tried to focus on work, thoughts of Iz floated around like they were anxious to land and take root. He couldn't think about her. He couldn't think about her creamy, smooth skin or how she'd feel to his touch. He threw himself into work, hit the gym every day if needed, and avoided seeing her as much as possible. That was his plan and hopefully, her attempts to grab his attention would magically disappear.

CHAPTER SIX

Friday morning, the texts from Chloe and Brianne started rolling in. Discussion about the plans and what to bring blew up her phone. Her friends would be expected by lunch. They could catch up and help Iz do more prep for the party. She was excited to see her friends. It had only been a week, but it felt longer. They were fun and a little crazy like Iz. She loved them like sisters.

She wanted to tell them about the infatuation—really, fixation—over Reed. She'd love to show them her new bikini he'd get to see when the time was right. But that discussion would have to wait.

Not that she expected any kind of judgment. Her friends knew firsthand about her adventurous and unreserved side. Iz was always the first to flash her boobs to earn her Mardi Gras beads, always first to kiss a stranger on a dare, always first to allow a boyfriend to play with her under the table at a restaurant. And her friends would almost always join in once Iz got the fun started.

Discussion of Reed might be premature at this point.

She drank some coffee and ate a bagel with cream cheese,

then returned to her bedroom to pick out an outfit, shower, and straighten her room. In no time, Brianne had arrived in her cute, old pale blue Bug. And before they even made it inside, Chloe pulled up.

"Ohmigosh, I missed you guys." Chloe looked beautifully tan.

"How was the cruise?" Iz asked.

They hugged, and the conversation started as they unloaded the cars and headed into the house.

The girls hustled upstairs and set down their luggage in the guestroom.

"Iz, if you had a large bed, we could all be in one room. Have a *real* slumber party," Brianne nearly bounced as she plopped on the bed and slipped off her sandals.

"Sorry, babe. The only king-sized bed in the house is Reed's."

"Ooh," Chloe said with a saucy grin.

"Oh, no, don't get her started," Brianne said with a grin.

"I can't help it. He's so hot."Chloe giggled at herself.

Izzy couldn't agree more.

"I know, but you missed something." Brianne turned to face Izzy. "What about your mom? You didn't say 'Reed and Mom's bed.'" Leave it to the criminal justice student to pick up on that.

"Yeah," Iz strung out the word. "I just learned they're getting a divorce."

"Oh, no," the ladies said in unison.

"I talked to Reed. He seems okay with it. And I met my mom this week. She's acting almost like she was never married."

"Wow." Brianne's eyes rounded.

"I'm so sorry." Chloe grabbed her hand. Brianne put an arm around her and squeezed.

"Thanks, y'all. I'm okay. I shouldn't have been too

surprised. But it's nice to hang here a little with Reed. Of course, he's working so much, I hardly see him, but I don't think that's gonna last." If Iz had anything to do with that.

"Okay, well, the plan this weekend is to eat, drink, and swim." Chloe looked at her two friends beaming.

"Perfect."

"So," Brianne unzipped her luggage and whipped out a hot pink floral bikini, "I followed your directions. I only packed bikinis and a toothbrush."

Iz grinned. "Okay, well, let's get 'em on, grab some lunch, and head out to the pool."

"I like the sound of that," Chloe chimed.

Thirty minutes later, the ladies were out back on loungers, large plastic bowls of salad in their hands. They spent the afternoon chatting over a pitcher of spiked Hawaiian Punch Iz had bought just for the occasion. None of them were big beer drinkers, but tootie-fruity drinks were just their speed. And she knew Reed wouldn't care if they raided his liquor cabinet.

Brianne shared that she already had some guy interested in her: a neighbor, home from college, who had played for their high school football team. According to Brianne, he matured and had now taken a liking to her. Chloe talked about her cruise and all the fun things she got to do, showing the girls her pictures from her phone.

By six o'clock, Reed had walked outside, pulling loose the tie around his neck. "Hello, ladies."

Ah, he was home. Iz smiled inside and out.

"Hello, Reed," they called to him.

"How about we have steak for dinner, ladies?"

"Yum," Chloe grinned up at him, a hand shielding her eyes from the sun.

"Do you need help?" Iz took in his dress slacks and crisp

button-down shirt. Reed belonged to a gym, and it showed. In his work clothes, he could be on the cover of GQ.

"I think I got it, but I'll let you know." He smiled and spun around, heading back into the house.

Chloe started. "Fuck, Iz. Is it just me, or has he gotten better looking?" she stage-whispered.

"It's true," Brianne chimed in.

"I have no idea what you're talking about." Iz shrugged a shoulder and rolled her eyes.

They all laughed because they knew she joked. He'd only gotten more handsome. Maybe that was the look of being stress-free now that his cheating wife had left. Whatever. He was handsome, smart, and confident. A winning combination.

An hour later, Reed had dinner served on the patio. The girls threw on cover-ups and took seats at the table. Everyone helped themselves to steak, potato salad, and a garden salad.

"Reed, I was thinking we could do burgers tomorrow. Would you be up for manning the grill?"

He grinned. "Sure."

They discussed the menu. Brianne volunteered to do macaroni salad, and Chloe said she'd make a few batches of brownies. Iz had dug out the string of clear lights to hang under the roof of the patio, and she thought she knew where to find tiny little American flags to stick in the yard. Everything was coming together.

"This is really good, Reed. Thanks."

"You're welcome."

As they finished dinner, Iz raced inside to retrieve a gallon of ice cream and four bowls.

"Oh, delish. My favorite brand."

It might be late, but for Iz and her girls, the night was still young.

As darkness fell, the ladies helped Reed clean up, then Izzy whipped up another pitcher of spiked punch.

"Okay, Iz, you got it from here?" Reed dried his hands with the kitchen towel.

"Yup. We're gonna hang out a while longer before heading to bed." She laid a hand on his shoulder for support, went on her tiptoes in her bare feet, and kissed him square on the mouth. Letting her torso press against his.

She wanted him addicted to her kisses, even if they were sorta platonic.

She lowered herself, smiled, and grasped the pitcher to walk out back.

Reed shook his head. Izzy was relentless with her kissing him. It occurred to him, at some point, she would give up. All the attention, the flirting, would go unrequited. She would likely get bored and find another guy to direct her attentions to for the summer.

He hung up the hand towel, turned off the overhead lights, leaving on the one over the sink, and headed to his office. He had a few small things to take care of. Then he'd retire to his bedroom, watch the news, and go to sleep.

From his office, he could hear the girls giggling. Thank goodness they didn't have close neighbors. At this hour, they might not appreciate the noise.

Shortly after, he switched off the desk lamp and headed upstairs. The screeching caught his attention again. Without flipping on the bedroom light, he hightailed it to the window.

Fuck!

He shouldn't have been surprised. Iz was skinny dipping with her friends. They looked like they were having fun, so carefree and basking in the beauty of youth. His sight couldn't leave Iz. Her smile, the bounce in her step, her playful nature with her girlfriends. He was drawn to her like no other woman. So full of life, it was almost contagious.

He'd been avoiding her, and he hated it. He didn't have a choice. It was for her own good. Being with him couldn't happen, and she would only get hurt in the end. One day, she would see he was protecting her.

But he wasn't dead. He was a man who could appreciate her beautiful body. Her delicate neck he could kiss. Her breasts he could cup. Her beautiful pussy he could make love to with his mouth. *If* she were his, he would know exactly how to please her, how to cherish her. Her pleasure would come first. He doubted any college guys she might date would understand that.

He sighed and walked away from the window. Sporting a hard-on was becoming habitual now and being around Iz was the reason.

This was going to be a long weekend.

CHAPTER SEVEN

Reed closed the cover of the grill he'd just scrubbed, grabbed his beer bottle, and sat in a chair pushed back from the table. Ah, his first chance to sit all night.

Everyone had eaten and now swam or lounged by the pool. Iz's white "Christmas" lights strung along the roofline sparkled against the dark night. Two of Iz's guy friends walked onto the covered patio, deep in the middle of some serious discussion.

"Reed," Mike started.

"Yes." He took a swig from his bottle.

"Maybe you can settle this." Ray pointed.

Iz came back outside from carrying in dirty plates and serving bowls. She rested a hand on the back of his chair, gazing at her friends.

"If a person doesn't fulfill their obligation of work—" Ray started.

"Like some kind of service you specifically hired them to do," Mike interjected.

"Can you stop payment on the check you gave them until the work is done to your satisfaction?" Ray asked.

Reed shook his head. "You can't do that."

Mike's eyes went wide. Ray only grinned.

"That's illegal. It's called check fraud. If you have an issue with incomplete work, you need to assign a value to that, and you can withhold *that* amount until the work is done."

"I knew it." Ray pumped his fist.

"Damn it." Mike slumped his shoulders in defeat.

Iz grinned and swung around to sit on Reed's lap. "My daddy's super smart." Then she pecked his lips.

"I told you." Ray sent Mike a shit-eating grin.

"That doesn't seem right. I think the law is wrong."

Reed smirked at the naiveté. Iz grinned and turned back to cup his cheek and kiss his lips again, this time much longer. Reed's breath caught and his fucking dick wanted to play along.

She broke the kiss and smiled.

"Your friends," Reed hissed between his teeth.

"Oh, they don't care," she replied, giving her head a little shake. Most of her friends knew she had a bold side.

Both the men turned and headed back to the poolside, the conversation seeming to take on a new direction of competitiveness.

She leaned in, skating her lips over his as her hand discreetly snaked between them to cup his growing erection.

He gripped her wrist, ceasing her audacious moves.

Her fingers caressed him. "One day, I would love to be down on my knees for you," she whispered over his lips, then she pulled on his bottom lip with her teeth. After one last peck, she rose and headed out to her friends hanging around the pool.

Fuck! That was an image! Iz down on her knees, taking his cock, was beyond anything he could hope for. He'd weave his fingers through that long hair, holding her while he fed his cock into her sassy mouth.

Fuck!

He drank from his beer, desperate to put out the fire burning inside him.

She was gorgeous and sweet, and she wanted him. It wasn't that he didn't want her, but he couldn't and he *shouldn't*. He was years older than her, and given their history, wouldn't a sexual relationship complicate things? Maybe even ruin things? He and Izzy had a great relationship the way it was. She was smart, funny, and just plain fun to be around.

He could see by the number of friends at his house they felt the same way. Iz had a magnetic personality. Focusing on that, and not how fucking amazing she would look naked, was the priority.

He glanced at his watch. Ten. He didn't know how long the party would go, but she was responsible. She could lock up.

Reed finished the last of his beer and turned to head to bed. If he didn't put some more distance between them, he was a doomed man.

CHAPTER EIGHT

The party had been a success. Everyone had a great time and had arranged rides or places to crash. Her besties, Chloe and Brianne, spent the night. They all had stayed up until the early morning talking and laughing. It felt great to connect with her friends without schoolwork looming over their heads.

Sunday, Iz and her friends cleaned inside while Reed cleaned outside. Then her friends left late Sunday afternoon.

She and Reed had a light dinner. Then after stacking the dishes, she decided to head to bed. She was wiped from a night of staying up late with her girls. Iz kissed him goodnight, lingering over his lips, of course. She loved kissing him, loved her lips on his. Maybe one day, he would pull her in and demand more than a closed-mouth kiss.

An idea popped in her head, and she called out from the bottom of the stairs. "I'll make chicken enchiladas tomorrow night for dinner." Those were one of his faves. She hoped he wouldn't hide out at work, but instead come home and eat with her.

Monday night, Reed came home late and had missed dinner. She could admit, it broke her heart. She wished he wouldn't shy away from her.

Should she say something?

At almost midnight, she heard him downstairs, followed shortly by the backdoor opening and closing.

Despite him avoiding her, that didn't change her fantasies. Her body and mind were not taking the hint.

And she fantasized not just about being in his bed. She'd dreamt about traveling, going out on dates, holding hands as they walked. She wanted it all. She didn't want to be alone.

She pulled back the bedsheet and strolled downstairs.

He sat in an oversized wicker chair, drinking a beer, staring out into the night.

"Hey."

"Hey." He looked up at her.

She strode to his spot, then sat on his lap, straddling him. "I missed you at dinner."

"Sorry." A hint of remorse showed in his eyes.

She paused a moment, and her arms circled his neck.

Instinctually, he wrapped his arms around her.

"I miss you when you work so much."

He didn't say anything, but she didn't expect him to.

She pressed closer, laying a head on his shoulder. She loved having her arms around him, and his arms drawing her in. She would never tire of being close to him—smelling him, feeling his heartbeat against her.

"Iz—"

She cut in. "I think about you. Fantasize, really," she whispered.

She heard a sharp intake by her ear.

"I don't quite know what to do with these feelings," she murmured then slowly pushed back, putting some air between them.

His hands rested on her hips.

Her gaze fell to his chest. She stroked her left hand over his chest, watching it rise and fall. She sighed and let her other hand slide from the back of his neck to her own chest, simultaneously feeling his heartbeat and hers.

She met his eyes as her hand roamed over her breast covered in a pale pink tank top. She caressed herself and toyed with her nipples, her head dropping back as she savored the sensations lighting her up.

The night was quiet. Only their breaths could be heard.

Her hand drifted lower, sliding under the wide leg of her boxers.

"Iz." His stern voice echoed in her ears, but she didn't stop.

"It feels so good. When I touch myself, I fantasize that it's you."

She circled her clit, moving the boxer fabric to make more room. The slickness didn't surprise her when she dipped inside.

She craved the thought of Reed pleasuring her. And just resting on his lap, smelling his masculine cologne, she could go there. If only for a little while, she could imagine Reed was the one bringing her this sweet pleasure.

The pressure built inside. She wished she was naked.

With her eyes closed, she rocked slightly and moaned, stroking a finger over her engorged clit while the other toyed with her nipples.

Please, watch me, she thought to herself.

"I want this finger to be yours. I dream about what you would feel like inside me." She moaned. "So good."

He gripped her hips and feeling him there—his warmth seeping into her—she came. She let go of the glorious sexual tension, bucking against her hand as she came on his lap. She moaned.

She pulled her head forward and collapsed over his shoulder, panting. *Incredible.*

Maybe next time, he could join her. She prayed he would.

As her breathing subsided, she pulled back, licked her lips, and found Reed watching her.

Gently, he lifted her as he stood, set her on the chair beside them, grabbed his bottle, and walked inside.

She slumped in her seat, the air leaving her lungs. Maybe that wasn't the smartest move.

After a few minutes, she entered the house and locked the door behind her. Climbing the stairs, she heard his shower water running.

She could cry, but she wouldn't. She refused. Her gut told her he felt it too. He wanted her just as much as she wanted him. She would have to exercise some patience. She had to believe he would come around. He would realize any sort of age gap was irrelevant. That they were meant to be together.

Motherfucker! How could he exist like this? Knowing Iz wanted him. Her sexy as fuck, feminine body open to receive him, eager and free. How does he hold back his aching cock? No, it was more than that. He had an ache to be with her. Be one in the way she wanted, and secretly, so did he. To talk and laugh like they used to.

The tepid water pummeled his body under the showerhead. Images of Iz on his lap replayed in his mind, sneaking her hand under the hem of her boxers. Her nipples had poked against her thin pink tank top. Her moans, her smell—she was so gorgeous, so free.

He'd held her through her orgasm and resisted anything more. He wanted to claim her, make her his. He wanted to give her everything she desired, but how?

It was impossible.

His fingers ran through his hair, sloshing water all over the shower walls. In a few quick tugs of his dick, he released *some* pent-up frustration, but it wasn't nearly enough.

She was beautiful when she came. He wanted to kiss her all over, taste her, bring her as much pleasure as her body could take.

He wasn't mad at her; it was nearly impossible to be mad at her. Even when she had run his car into the garage door or ruined his favorite white T-shirt in the laundry, he wasn't mad. He adored that girl, now a woman. He wanted only the best for her. He only questioned if the best included him.

He shut off the water and toweled off. "Iz, what am going to do about you?" he muttered into the empty space, hoping a solution might present itself.

CHAPTER NINE

A few days had passed since the late night patio event with Reed. She hadn't seen him much; he was still avoiding her. She'd still cooked for both of them, and most nights Reed would reheat the dinner and eat before retiring to his room.

She'd asked him, "Seems like you're really busy these days."

He'd replied, "Yes." And that was it.

She knew the truth, though. He was hiding from her—unable to tell her yes, but unable to tell her no.

Thursday morning, Iz awoke with the most brilliant idea. A full plan slowly unfolded in her little head. It was risky, but Reed was worth the risk.

She grabbed a to-go cup of coffee and headed to the store. She got the fixings for one of his favorite dishes, chicken parmigiana, and a boutique of flowers because she thought they were pretty and smelled great.

She leisured back at the house over another cup of coffee and a croissant, then pampered herself from head-to-toe after her shower. Her skin glowed with the sun she'd gotten.

Phone in hand, she practiced several poses in front of the mirror, finally deciding on one. *Perfect.*

Holding her breath, she added a caption and sent it.

Holy crap! Her heart skipped a beat.

That could have been the best decision she'd ever made or the worst. She became lightheaded.

"You have to know, Iz," she told her reflection. "Win, lose, or draw. You want him, and now he knows it."

She slipped on her new mini bikini in the hopes that he would get to see her in it...and she prayed this was the day. The following day, she'd start her new job and wouldn't see him until dinnertime.

Dressed, she grabbed her sunglasses, suntan lotion, and her phone and headed out back to the pool.

Reed sat in the conference room with the head of production, Ed Brinkley, and a few of his team members, reviewing the particulars of the patent infringement lawsuit he was about to file. This was a huge case for GS&M. One they could not afford to lose. Although their chances of winning were high, no detail could be ignored.

His phone buzzed in his pocket. Honestly, he didn't get many calls on his cell because he preferred to have Nikia, his admin, field his calls and personally call or text him if something was urgent. Otherwise, she'd collect messages that he could attend to once the meeting was over.

It was from Izzy. His brows pulled together. He opened the message...

Holy fuck!

He glanced up briefly as the others discussed a particular point that might not be necessary for the filing.

He swallowed hard and glanced back down at his lap.

She'd sent him a nude picture. Her hands covered her lady

parts. One hand stretched across her chest allowed some areola to peek through.

His cock came alive.

He shifted in his seat and glanced at the group again. Zero attention was being paid to him. But still, this was an incredibly inappropriate place for a hard-on.

Beads of sweat formed over his upper lip.

The text read: *I'm making your favorite dinner tonight. Please join me. I miss you.*

Iz was gorgeous, no doubt about it.

"What do you think, Reed?"

He looked up at Ed across the table from him, his heart still racing. "I'm sorry. What was the question?"

"We wondered if the in-production or just the ship dates for the T-32 should be included in the suit paperwork."

He shook his head slowly, forcing his mind back on business. "The Complaint is really a short, plain statement. Usually, a lot of detail is not required at this point."

Ed nodded. His colleagues went back to their topic, but Reed had a sense they were really done at this point. Besides, the rise in his blood pressure from a saucy twenty-year-old was too much for him to handle right then. He needed to address this once and for all.

"Folks, I think I have everything I need for the filing at this point. Let's reconvene same time next week and finish gathering the meat of what we need should this case go to court." He rose, everyone taking his cue and rising too.

"Thanks for everything, Reed. We spent years developing this chip. The thought of someone profiting off our hard work pisses me off."

He gave Ed an understanding smile and shook his hand. "You're welcome. See you next week."

Reed spun around and headed straight to his office.

"Nikia, something's come up that I need to take care of.

Would you please reschedule my afternoon appointments for later?"

"Sure, Reed. See ya' tomorrow."

Reed pulled into the garage, reminding himself Iz meant no harm. She thought she could get what she wanted from him. He would exercise some patience because, truly, she was a sweetheart.

He'd handle the matter like he would a work situation—calm, cool, and collected.

The fact was her texts were distracting, and if he didn't squash it now, well...

His blood pressure shot up again. He loosened his tie and undid his top button. He took in a deep breath and entered the house through the laundry room. Turning the corner, he stepped into the kitchen.

Iz stood with her back to the door, pouring lemonade into a plastic cup. She wore a skimpy thong bikini.

"What the hell, Iz?"

She screeched, jumped, and spun around. Some lemonade splashed onto the counter. "Gosh, Reed! You scared the crap out of me." Her hand went to her heart.

Fuck! The front of her suit was just as skimpy as the back. The white confection barely covered her nipples as she'd scrunched the top over each breast, and the bottoms had the tiniest piece of fabric covering her pussy lips.

He stalked closer. The tongue-lashing he'd been prepared to give her escaped his mind. He was so distracted, and his hard dick didn't help matters.

A foot away from her, he stopped and glowered over her. "This so-called swimsuit covers less than your hands did." He referred to the text picture she sent him an hour earlier.

She swallowed.

"I should spank you for sending me that text *and* for parading around in such a skimpy outfit."

"You've never spanked me before." Her voice barely above a whisper.

"Maybe this is a good time to start."

She didn't say a word, just held his gaze. Her blue doe eyes trusting him.

He inched closer, unable to resist skimming his fingertips over the straps of her bathing suit top. He quietly asked, "What am I going to do about you?" more for himself than for her.

Her tanned skin warmed his fingertips. Her breasts moved under his touch as her breathing accelerated.

He slipped just the tip of his index finger under the garment, slowly skimming up and down, likely glossing over some pink areola.

"So smooth." He wasn't sure if he'd said the words or just thought them.

Out of curiosity of what lies beneath, he lifted the swimsuit top to the sides, revealing her breasts. He sucked in a breath.

Her breasts were perfectly ripe, like succulent summer fruit. He skimmed his thumbs over her pink nipples, watching them pucker with the intimate contact.

Iz's lips gaped, her gentle breath flowing in the space between them.

She fascinated him; it was that simple.

He was drawn to her and found it impossible to tear himself away. His fingers played, and he watched color rise in her cheeks. He had to taste. He leaned down to lave and suck at a pink nipple while his hands laid a trail over the smooth skin of her torso.

She mewled and arched into him.

Driven for still more, he crouched down and inhaled her

delicate scent. His fingertips danced over the fabric just covering her mound. The suit had barely enough fabric to cover her slit and lips.

She whimpered.

He knew what she wanted. Still gliding a finger over the tiny rectangle of fabric, he considered his next move. Although he couldn't give her *everything*, he could at least ease her ache.

Without any internal debate, Reed peeled down her tiny string bikini bottoms a few inches. *Fuck me!*

Her arousal stuck to the inside of her suit. And her pussy was smooth and nude. He'd gotten a glimpse of her Friday night—but up close... The sight before him was breathtaking.

Glossing a finger over her smooth lips caused a sharp intake, and her head fell back.

Gazing up at her, he asked, "Do you want to come?"

She licked her lips. "Yes. Please."

With both hands, he slid off her bikini bottoms and commanded, "Up on the table."

She climbed onto the large wooden dining table and sat facing him, her beautiful face flushed.

He reached behind and pulled free the white bikini top, leaving her glowing, tanned, naked body completely nude and exposed to him.

"Swing your calves underneath you and lay back."

She maneuvered her feet under her ass, one leg at a time. Then she slowly lowered her body back to lay flat on the table.

His cock jerked behind his pants' zipper.

She was so damn flexible and positively stunning in this position.

God, she looked so enticing, offering herself to him.

Reed loved how her clit poked out, reaching for him. He spread her knees a few more inches apart. "Gorgeous."

He leaned down and blew a gentle breath over her sex.

"Ah. God, Reed."

Her arousal slid past her lips. One of the more beautiful things he'd ever seen.

He captured some of it with a fingertip and swirled it over her clit.

"Unh." She bucked slightly at the contact.

"Why don't you have a boyfriend, Iz?"

She sighed. "I don't want a boy. I want a man."

Hm. He played a while longer until he couldn't take it anymore. He leaned down and tongued her clit.

"Oh, God. Yes, Reed." She moaned, her hips flexing to meet his mouth.

He loved how she called to him. The anger from the earlier text now completely dissipated. Caught up in the moment, he could only see making Iz cry out his name with a climax he'd given her.

He swiped again as he pinned her thighs down.

Her skin was soft and warm. Her entire body was delicious. He could stay there all day.

He reached his hands up to cup her breasts and toy with her nipples.

She moaned long and low. She was close.

His tongue worked her slit and poked inside, lapping at her smooth lips on the way up. Reclaiming her clit, the first of her tremors started.

He twirled over her hot button as he slid two fingers inside her wet pussy.

So fucking incredible.

She pulled on his fingers as the climax took over. Her back bowing off the table while she screamed out his name.

The orgasm lasted longer than he'd ever experienced with a woman.

She took a few moments, air filling her lungs. She opened her hazy eyes and met his gaze.

He rose, pulled out his fingers, and stared at the beautiful naked body before him. If he had a blanket, he'd force himself to cover her so the image wouldn't be so tantalizing.

She pushed into an upright position and reached for his belt.

He grabbed her wrist, stopping the motion.

"I just want to feel you. Please let me feel you." She unfastened him with her other hand.

Shit! She was too fast.

Her left hand reached inside his briefs and cupped his granite-hard dick.

He groaned. *Fuck!*

Her warm hand was incredible wrapped around him. She stroked him gently as her other hand pushed his pants and underwear out of the way and down his thighs.

She shimmied closer to him, her knees off the edge of the table. She lowered his cock, pointing him between her legs.

"Iz." He knew what she wanted, and she damn-near begged him with her eyes.

With one hand braced behind her, she lifted her hips closer to him. "Enter me, Reed. Please. I want you to feel the love I have for you," she whispered.

She raised her hips another inch, arching as far as she could. He leaned forward, making contact with her wet slit.

She gently pulled on him, coaxing him closer.

He pushed, his head slipping inside, and she moaned. He went another inch and another, until he was fully seated inside her. She came instantly, squeezing his dick, wrapping him in a warm blanket of passion.

She moaned, and her head fell back. *Amazing.*

He gathered all the strength he had to not climax.

As her breathing calmed, she opened her eyes.

He backed away a fraction when she grabbed the back of his neck.

"Stay."

"If I stay, I'll explode," he confessed.

"I just finished my period."

He exhaled.

She couldn't get pregnant, and he would bet she was clean. After he learned of Miranda's shenanigans, he got tested. He was clean.

Feeling her heat wrapped around him, how could he leave? He didn't want to stay but leaving sounded worse. She was so tight, so silky warm. He had to do something.

He moved, pushing and pulling once, then he leaned over her and kissed her precious mouth. His tongue dove deep into the recesses of her welcoming mouth. He groaned.

It felt like heaven buried deep inside her. He pumped more, desperate to hold on just a few moments longer.

Iz panted. "Yes, Reed. Oh, God, Reed. You feel so good."

Like a man possessed, he thrust deeper, and together they rocked on the table. A twitch from her pussy muscles gripped his dick.

Fuck! She was going to come again.

She did. She gripped him tight, detonating his own orgasm.

He blew his seed inside her, coming for what seemed like an eternity, electricity shooting to every square inch of his being. Finally, he collapsed over her, panting into her neck, hearing her rapid breaths at his ear.

Slowly, reality returned and hit him like a ton of bricks.

What the fuck did I just do?

He pushed off the table, meeting her lust-filled gaze.

He pulled out. "You got what you wanted. Now, no more texts at work," his voice rasped. He swooped down, yanked up his pants, and headed out the garage door.

What had he done? He couldn't get out of there fast enough.

Chapter Ten

Iz hadn't seen Reed all night. He'd left after their escapade on the kitchen table, and she hadn't seen him since. It was nearly midnight. Her heart ached.

Making love to Reed had been so incredible. Like nothing she'd ever experienced before. The vision of his broad shoulders between her legs, the feel of his expert tongue on her, all of it made her heart soar with the intimacy they shared.

After they'd made love, she thought he was hooked. He'd kissed her and made her come several times. What more proof did he need that they belonged together? Instead of taking her to his bed, he'd left, probably sitting in a bar, beating himself up over the whole incident.

As she got ready for bed, she heard the rumble of the garage door. He was home.

She stared at her reflection, looking for an answer. She had to do something. She couldn't let it lie like this between them.

She knew Reed, not just his Virgo, neat-freak tendencies. She knew his little quirks, like how he'd put on his seatbelt after he got moving. Or how he'd only get really mad when people didn't use their heads. She knew how mixing a fresh jar of natural peanut butter frustrated him, but he wouldn't have it any other way.

She also knew Reed was too good for Miranda. She loved her mother but could say that with a hundred percent confidence. He deserved someone who worshipped him, appreciated all he had to offer and could love him like no other woman on the planet.

Iz knew in her heart she was that woman.

She crawled into bed and lay there for several long minutes, staring into the darkness.

That's it! She sighed, and after pulling back the covers, she stripped out of her clothes and walked the hall to his bedroom.

In the dim moonlight, she saw him lying on his side in bed. She pulled back the sheet and slid in behind him—behind his warm and naked body. She didn't know he slept that way. The thrill sent a flood of lust racing through her. She caressed his arm and back and peppered kisses on the back of his neck and in between his shoulder blades. Her hand caressed down his torso to his hips and ass.

"Iz," he murmured in his sleepy state.

She didn't stop. With her naked body pressed against his, she slid a hand up his chest, gripping his incredible pecs. She intentionally avoided his cock, although if his shallow breathing were any indication, he was hard. Hard for *her*.

"I love you. I've always loved you, and now it's so much more. I meant it when I said I can't imagine my life without you in it."

She gently pushed him onto his back, shifted upright, and pulled the sheet back. He didn't protest, but he didn't touch her either.

She gazed down at him. "I don't want *one and done*."

He met her gaze, then his sight traveled the length of her.

She stroked his chest slowly. "We have always had a

connection, from the very day we met. Regardless of where this goes, that will never change. I know you love me—"

"Iz, it's different."

"It *was* different. I was a child, I was your stepdaughter, and you were married to my mother. *Now*, what we have is deeper; it's so much more." She kissed his chest and caressed his upper arms.

"I want you. I want no other man but you. I wanna feel you inside me, and I know you want that too. You're as hard as a rock, and I haven't even touched you there." She swung her leg around to straddle his waist but remained hovering over him. She reached for his two hands and raised them up to her breasts. "I love and adore you, Reed. I know you feel the same way. Show me, Reed. Show me how much I mean to you."

For the first time since she crawled into his bed, she touched his cock. He groaned. It was thick and strong.

She kept his gaze as she held him, hovering her pussy above him. Waiting for him to object or throw her off, there was nothing. Nothing but the sound of their heavy breathing.

Trembling with lust, she lowered herself, slowly, taking him in inch by inch. When he was completely buried, they both moaned. The connection was amazing.

His hands gripped her hips.

"Oh, God, Reed." Her head dropped back.

His thickened cock pushed against her walls, flooding her body with anticipation and satisfaction of having him inside her. Divine. But she had to wait for him.

As she moved slowly over him, she bent forward, chest to chest, and pressed her lips to his.

Nipping him and running her tongue along his lower lip, he opened for her. She dove in, claiming her man, showing him how she adored him. Telling him no other woman would love and appreciate him like her.

He cupped her head and plumbed her depths, connecting with her in as many ways as humanly possible.

Swiftly, he twisted and swung over her, trapping her beneath him. His thrusts went wild as he continued his deep kiss, his arms pulling her tight into him.

She circled him with her legs, then cupped his head and broke their kiss. "Come with me. Come in me."

Her tremors started, and she couldn't stop them. Her orgasm gripped him.

He growled, and in a few short beats, came inside her, panting into the crux of her neck.

Her arms wrapped around him, riding the wave of her incredible orgasm and savoring the feel of his skin against hers, of his heart beating with hers.

They held onto each other when finally, he raised his head, his expression unreadable. She looked up at him but didn't say a word. A hint of panic skipped her heart.

"I tried to fight it." He blinked, not yet pulling out.

"I know." She stroked the side of his jaw.

She held her breath, fearing they were done. Fearing he would tell her to go, that they couldn't do this again.

"Iz."

She bit on her lip.

"I never knew it could be like this."

She nodded slowly.

"I don't want to be with anyone else either."

Did she hear that right?

A smile slowly formed on his lips.

The pressure began to build again inside as he grew in her wet channel. Tears pricked the back of her eyes.

"Reed." She pulled his head down to kiss him. Her lips tilted over his, letting the kiss build slowly just as his thrusts built inside her. "I love you," she breathed over his lips. "I want you for as long as you'll have me."

Her orgasm quickly gained momentum, in a shocking way, crashing through her, causing her to cry out. "Ah."

He never stopped making love to her, never broke their precious connection.

She threaded her fingers through his hair. "Please don't avoid me," she pleaded. "Please don't stay all day at work. Come home to me."

He nodded, and after a short pause, he said, "I want you in my bed from now on. I will love you the way you deserved to be loved."

His words were sweet music to her ears. Another tear escaped as the emotion overwhelmed her.

He claimed her lips again, and his speed increased.

She came again, screaming into his mouth as she clutched his shoulders.

She'd waited to hear those words. She hadn't known how deeply she felt about Reed, but once the spark of recognition was there, she couldn't ignore it. Some might say it was wrong, but she didn't care.

He hadn't stopped moving. He kissed her until another climax exploded around him, sucking him further in.

Although she'd only had a few boyfriends, she'd never been with a man who could make her come so much. And just from moving inside her.

"Fuck, Iz. I love how you grip me when you come. I love seeing you come and knowing I'm doing that to you."

"Yes, you, Reed. No one else."

He kept moving inside her and bringing out orgasm after orgasm. He kissed her swollen lips, her face, her neck, not stopping his delicious thrusts. God, he had the stamina of a workhorse.

Iz felt the wet spot on the bed growing beneath them, but she didn't think either one of them cared. All she knew was she didn't want this night to end.

After making passionate love to Iz, Reed released his seed deep inside her, letting go all the anxiety, remorse, and regret from the past several years. It was like a sense of peace had fallen over him he'd been waiting an eternity to find.

He pulled out, retrieved a towel to clean what he could, and held her close as they dosed off.

He didn't know how long they could be together, but he knew right then, it was perfect. She was perfect.

He wanted to please her—in bed and out. He wanted to give and buy her anything she wanted. She was his to cherish. Her feisty little persistence showed him that.

They would have to keep their relationship hushed, but that wouldn't be too hard.

Someday, she would find a man whom she'd marry and give her babies. Until that time came, Reed would show her what it was like to be loved, respected, and cherished as she rightly deserved. She should be worshipped. Her body should be worshipped.

He awoke hard for her. Of course, it didn't help that she lay exactly as she'd fallen asleep—naked and in his arms.

He kissed her neck and back, rousing her gently.

"Reed," she breathed out.

"Yes, baby." He kissed and licked her sweet skin. "You start your new job today, right?"

"Mmhm."

He wedged his leg between hers and nestled his dick at the apex of her legs. "Then, I need to fuck you now to get me through the day," he whispered in her ear.

He caressed her breasts, loving the soft moans escaping her mouth.

"Baby, we need to keep this between you and I, you know that, right?"

After a quick test with his finger, he easily pushed into her tight, wet channel and groaned.

She arched and reached her arms overhead, clasping the back of his head. "Yes, Daddy."

Oh, that was new. He actually kinda liked it.

He massaged a finger over her clit, giving her two orgasms before he released himself.

Lying still inside her, he was a man on top of the world. Maybe he should be scolding himself for not turning her away. But having her here in his bed, in his arms, he never felt so right, so at peace.

"I love you, Daddy."

"I love you too, baby."

He slipped out of her, and she rolled onto her back to meet his gaze. "You'll be home for dinner?"

He smiled. "Yes, I'll make dinner. You can tell me all about your day when you come home."

She beamed up at him.

He pecked her lips and slid out of bed to get ready for work. And for the first time in a long time, he couldn't wait to get back home.

Chapter Eleven

Izzy's new job was waitressing at a family-owned Italian restaurant that had been in the area for years. Generations of Coppolas had owned the business and grew it. The tables were decked with white tablecloths and votive candles, and the walls were decorated with autographed stars that had patronized the restaurant over the years. The whole place lingered with mouthwatering scents. She wondered how everyone wasn't overweight who worked there.

She met two other waitresses, Joy and Brenda, the head chef, Jesus, and Mr. Coppola's wife and his nephew, Robert. She shadowed Joy for a while, then was given her own tables. Nothing too challenging, and she caught on quickly for most things. Everyone was so nice, and she was thankful for their patience. Like when she confused a linguini order with a fettuccini order. Or when she kept mispronouncing bruschetta.

"It's bruschetta. Pretend there's a K in there," Mr. Coppola said with his subtle Italian accent. "Like chianti is 'key-anti', instead of 'chee-anti'." The way he spoke, with his fingers pinched together and waving in the air, she couldn't help but smile. She knew she'd made the right choice working at Coppola's.

Working the lunch hour was probably a walk in the park compared to the dinner hours. Her first dinner shift was two days away. This shift was mostly for training.

Iz pocketed some decent tips which brought a smile to her face. Although she had money Reed would put in her account, she took pride in earning her own spending money.

Reed.

She was so busy she hardly had a chance to think about him. In the afternoon, she clocked out, hopped in her little import that Reed bought her for graduation, and headed home. She couldn't wait to see him.

Reed's phone rang an hour before he expected Izzy.

Miranda.

"Miranda, I'm surprised to hear from you."

"Reed, how are you?"

Like she really cared. "I'm fine." His blood pressure rose. He knew he shouldn't have answered the call. "What did you call for, Miranda?"

She sighed heavily. "You know I did try, Reed. It wasn't all my fault."

What? "What part? The cheating? The arguing? The unadventurous sex?" His blood pressure was rising by the second.

"I wanted to be happy with you, Reed. I did." Her pause was so long, he knew she wasn't going to say what she was implying.

"So, what you're saying is I didn't make you happy. Is that right? I drove you to cheat?"

Another dramatic sigh. "It takes two to have a relationship. And I *tried* to make you happy."

The hell you did.

"But that's not why I called. My condo is a great place, but it's not cheap. I need you to send some money to my account."

"Wait a minute. You're making money."

"I don't make as much as you?"

"So, you have no problem spending my money, but you won't spend your own?"

"It's not that. And aside from that, you have a mortgage. That stays the same. I have rent payments that can go up. I think we need to reevaluate this. I'm trying to think long-term."

"Uh-huh."

"All I'm asking is for you to revisit the numbers. Then I'll be ready to sign."

"I'll see what I can do." He was done with this conversation. "Anything else?"

"Uh, no."

"Okay, goodbye." And he ended the call. He took several deep breaths, willing calm to seep into his body and allowing him to put a smile back on his face and not think about Miranda.

A short time later, Izzy walked into the kitchen from the garage with a smile on her face. She looked adorable dressed in her black pants and apron with her white, button-down top, giving just enough room for her beautiful tits without pulling against it.

"Daddy!" She raced to him and jumped in his arms.

He kissed her with fervor. The conversation with Miranda vanishing by the second. He hated to admit it, but he missed her. Thoughts of Iz would pop in his mind, distracting him, but also making him feel so fucking alive.

When was the last time he'd felt this good?

Pulling back and looking into her twinkling blue eyes, he spoke, "How was your first day?"

"Great. Everyone's so nice. I really think I'm gonna like it."

"Good for you. Dinner is basically ready. It's not too hot. How about we eat outside tonight?"

"Sounds great."

"Okay, I'm gonna check on the barbeque chicken. I have a call to make. How about you set the table?"

"Okay." She pecked his lips one last time and went about gathering plates, silverware, and placemats.

He extinguished the fire from the grill, set the chicken on a plate, and covered it. Then he headed to his office to call his attorney.

"Phillip. I hope this isn't a bad time."

"Not at all. What's going on, Reed?" He heard an exhale like Phillip was smoking a cigarette.

"I just wanted to touch base. I got a call from Miranda earlier today."

"What the hell? She's supposed to go through her lawyer. *All* communication."

"I know." Reed really didn't want to think about that woman anymore. He realized the mistake he'd made in marrying her, and if he was to marry again, he'd be a lot more astute about what he was getting himself into. The best thing about his marriage was having sweet, vivacious Izzy in his life.

"What did she want?" Phillip's voice reeked of frustration. "More money?"

"Of course." Reed ran a hand down the back of his neck.

Phillip started. "Look, it's a good settlement. And we don't have to cave on anything. I don't want you giving away too much just to get her out of your life. Okay?"

Reed sighed. "Yup."

"All right. I'll reach out and let you know what I hear."

"Thanks, Phillip. I appreciate it." He disconnected the line and stared into the empty space. Moving on with his life that didn't include Miranda was paramount. Reed wondered if she ever really loved him or if it was all an act. Was she even capable of a committed, loving relationship?

Iz walked in wearing a cut-off T-shirt and short denim skirt. "Daddy, are you done? Can we eat?"

He smiled at his baby girl. She was like a ray of sunshine.

"Yes, I'm done now."

She approached, resting a hand on the back of the chair and smiling down at him.

"What is it?" he asked.

"I was just wondering. Does your admin ever call in sick?"

"Sometimes, but it doesn't happen very often. Why?"

Iz had a twinkle in her eye. "Because if she does, I want to come in and substitute for her. I fantasize about you calling me into your office and bending me over your desk."

Oh fuck! He stroked a hand down her arm. "Baby, that would be incredible. I'll keep that in mind. Although if you were outside my office, I'd find it very hard to get any work done."

She grinned and leaned down to kiss his lips.

"C'mon, let's go eat."

He took her hand, and they strode out to the patio. She'd set the table with placemats, plates, and silverware, and dishes of the potato salad and bean salad. She'd also brought an open bottle of white wine and a stemmed glass for him.

Reed loved wine, had it every night. For some reason, lately he'd had less of a desire for drinking. Maybe because he had desires for other things.

The evening temperature was perfect for sitting outside. They ate and talked mostly about her new job. He made a mental note to swing by someday when she was working, maybe for lunch.

Iz asked about the status of the divorce; perhaps she overheard some of his conversation with Phillip.

"It's going. This can be a slow process." He sipped from

his wineglass. "Iz, when you're looking to get married, don't rush it. Get to know the man well, make sure you have a lot in common, and make sure you like him. Like he's also your friend."

She nodded thoughtfully. "I will. But I have time."

"You do."

She leaned closer and kissed below his ear. "I want a man like you. One who treats me with respect and knows how to please me. In and out of bed." She licked up the side of his neck and gently bit on his skin.

She pushed back. "Do you want to swim?"

Without waiting for an answer, she rose and stripped off her tee and skirt, revealing her beautiful body clad in the skimpy bathing suit he'd seen just a few days prior.

"Fuck, Iz."

His girl was incorrigible.

Iz couldn't explain it; she needed him all the time. Stepping closer, she wiggled her way to straddle Reed's lap.

He quickly rested his wine on the table and gripped her hips. "You're gorgeous."

"Did you know I bought this for you?" She referred to the bikini.

His head tilted. "I didn't."

She played with the triangle top, slowly shifting the fabric to unveil more skin. "I won't wear this for anyone but you."

Her hand reached behind her back and pulled free the string holding the top in place. She whipped it up over her head and dropped it to the ground.

He glanced to the left and right, likely checking if neighbors were near. With the lot size of the houses in this area, it was improbable.

"Good. It's sexy. And I love that it's for my eyes only." His hands slid up her torso to cup her breasts. Then he lifted her by her ribcage to bring a nipple to his mouth, one at a time he savored their deliciousness.

She loved how he'd just claim her whenever he wanted.

She stood over and let him roam freely.

"You want me to fuck you out here, don't you?" He stroked her torso and her ass.

"Yes, Daddy."

He slid a hand up her thigh to her mound, dipping a finger under the tiny scrap of fabric covering her pussy. She was wet. As he pushed a finger inside, her head fell back. He pulsed and twisted his finger before glossing it over her engorged clit.

With his free hand, he unfastened his shorts, springing free his eager cock. He could take her any time of the day.

Pulling the bikini out of the way was easy. There was so much give in the fabric, this suit was made for one thing and one thing only.

Lining herself up, he guided her down. They both moaned.

"Daddy." She breathed out.

"You feel incredible, baby girl. I can't get enough of you."

"Daddy, I'm on the pill. You can have me whenever you want."

During the short time she'd dated Josh, he had always used condoms. By the time she got around to visiting the school's clinic for a prescription for birth control, they'd broken up. That pack of pills had been sitting in the bottom of her purse ever since. The prior Sunday morning knowing her period was finished, she took the first pill.

His eyes rounded. He gripped the back of her neck, bringing her mouth to his.

She rocked over him, riding him as he gently twirled his

finger over her clit. The first orgasm raced to the surface, and she gripped his shoulders as the sensations consumed her.

She leaned forward and, gripping his head, she kissed him. Her tongue toiled with his, reaching for more, showing him he was all she wanted right then.

"Daddy," she panted, "come with me. Please."

"Yes, baby girl."

She continued rocking, and at the first muscle pulse around his cock, he released, letting his seed pummel her insides. They moaned simultaneously, gripping each other, riding the waves of ecstasy.

"Baby, you're beautiful."

She smiled and leaned down to kiss him again—languid and sensual—she was far from done with him.

He gazed up at her. "Let's clean up and take this to the bedroom."

CHAPTER TWELVE

Friday morning, shortly after getting settled at his desk at work, Reed called his long-time friend, really his best friend, Kyle.

"Man, how are you? Long time."

"Yeah, sorry. Life's been crazy." *That was an understatement*, Reed thought. "Got time tonight to grab a drink?"

"Yeah, sounds good. Where to?"

"How about Massimo's at five?"

"Perfect. See ya' then."

Reed disconnected the line. He and Kyle were friends since shortly after college, and together they'd climbed the ladders of success in each of their careers. Reed's path had been much more crooked than Kyle's.

Kyle had seen Reed at his great moments *and* his less than shining moments. Before finally maturing and settling down with Miranda, Reed had a wild streak in him. He'd acted like he had something to prove, but it was far from productive. Drinking, occasional drugs, and sex. Reed'd loved it all, from fast cars to fast women. One DUI hadn't slowed him down. One close-call pregnancy when he was twenty-three hadn't slowed him down. But when he wrecked his sports car driving hungover and broke three ribs, *that* had slowed him down.

Kyle had been his friend through it all. He'd said *Man, you gotta course-correct because these things won't fix themselves. And it could definitely get worse.*

Shortly after life had come to a staggering halt, Reed cleaned himself up, received promotions and raises at work, and met Miranda and Izzy. It might have taken some time, but he'd put his law degree to work and turned his life around.

Meeting Miranda and Izzy opened Reed's heart to a world of possibilities. He'd never forget the incredible feeling that came over him when he met Izzy. Those big blue eyes looked up at him like he was her hero.

He realized looking back he was more in love with the idea of being in love, of being surrounded by family. He had turned a corner in life, cleaned himself up, and picked himself up by his bootstraps. He knew he could commit to relationship, and he was anxious to start that next chapter of life. His newfound openness and willingness to embrace life had caused him to make the leap and marry Miranda. He also knew part of it was falling in love with this sweet little brown haired, blue-eyed girl.

With these new developments—this change in his relationship with Iz—Reed needed his friend. Someone to give him insight when he was questioning his next move.

At five, Reed strolled into the bar and quickly saw Kyle sitting at a high table in the back corner.

"Hey, man. Good to see ya'." Reed embraced his friend and took a seat.

Kyle had already ordered beer for both of them, and in a quick minute, a waitress with short, spiked hair and ruby red lips delivered them.

"Cheers." Kyle held up his mug.

"Cheers."

Reed asked what was new in his friend's life, and the conversation flowed. His friend looked happy—smiling when he talked about Rochelle and the kids. They recently put in a pool, and the kids were like fish, swimming whenever they had a free moment.

Kyle was a good father.

"So, tell me what's new with you. How're Miranda and Izzy?"

He took a swig from his mug. "Miranda and I are getting a divorce."

Kyle rested a hand on his shoulder. "Aw, shit, man. I'm sorry."

"It's okay. I think she may actually be happier single. Able to date whomever she wants." Reed sipped from his glass.

"But what about you? Are you happier?" He pinned Reed with a look.

"Honestly, the break-up isn't as hard as I thought it was going to be. I don't know, I guess I thought after seven years I'd have a more visceral response." He exhaled. "'Course, maybe having another distraction is the reason."

Kyle grinned and lifted his brows. "Another distraction?"

Reed swallowed hard. "You're not gonna believe this but Iz and I are seeing each other."

Kyle was silent for a while. "Okay."

Reed glanced at his friend. "Okay?"

Kyle shrugged. "She's not your biological daughter. Aren't you allowed to see whomever you want?"

Now, it was Reed's turn to be surprised. "Sure, but the age difference is pretty huge."

"I get that. Are you two getting along?"

Reed nodded.

"This doesn't have to be forever, right?" Kyle asked before flagging down the waitress for refills.

Reed shook his head. "No, but... I guess I thought you'd tell me to let it go."

"I'm not gonna judge you." He grinned as if a memory had popped into his head. "You and Iz have always had a great connection. She's always been the apple of your eye."

Reed smiled, the thought warming him from the inside. "You're exactly right. Part of me thinks I proposed to Miranda because I wanted to whole package—a loving family, a house in suburbia with a white picket fence." He ran a hand down the back of his neck. "I guess...given my history..." He paused, unable to say the words aloud.

"You were wondering if this was like all those other women."

Reed chewed the inside of his cheek. "Man, you know I've chased women, they chased me. We always had a good time. That was my life—my motto—for years. 'Have a good time.'"

Kyle brows furrowed. "You think that's what this is between you and Iz?"

His head whipped toward his friend. "No. Of course, not. I mean, maybe. It could be." He wiped a hand over his mouth and jawline. He didn't think he was using Iz—his stomach roiled at the idea—but she was young...

Kyle sighed. "Man, I think you can take a breather. This isn't like when you were out carousing, sowing your oats and shit. That phase of your life is gone. You're forty-six. You've matured. If you have an attraction and feelings for Iz, it's probably because they're real." He patted Reed on the back. "I don't think you need to beat yourself up about it."

Reed lifted his head. Maybe his friend was right. Reed would never degrade Iz in that way. When he was younger, he was an asshole, probably broke a few hearts. He could honestly say he would never intentional hurt Izzy. Not even if his life depended on it.

"All you need to do is make sure you're both clear on what you have and what she expects long-term. At some point, she's gonna want to get married and probably have babies."

He nodded. "And I can't be that for her."

He nodded. "That's right. In the meantime, if you're both going into this open-eyed," he tipped his head, "have fun."

A smile pulled at the corners of Reed's lips. "That's an understatement. She's insatiable," he confessed. "Maybe I am too."

"It's called hormones, bro. She's got all hers in spades." Kyle smirked as he sipped on his beer.

"I won't make you jealous with the details, but I can hardly keep my hands off her. Beyond that, she sweet and caring, always thinking about me. It's been a long, damned time since I've felt this good."

"Good for you." Kyle grinned.

At the risk of staying on this topic any longer and sounding like a horny teenager, Reed changed the subject. Hearing his friend's wise words was all he needed to get peace of mind.

Reed knew he wouldn't hold Iz back. She had her whole life ahead of her. When the time was right, he would set her free to pursue her happily-ever-after. He himself might be ready to get back into the dating world too.

In his heart he knew, she would always be the apple of his eye. Nothing was going to change that.

Amazing how in just a few short days the world could look so entirely different. Iz was dancing on the clouds. Spending time with Reed in their new relationship filled her in unexpected ways. Iz had always had an adventurous side, sure. Anyone who knew her knew risk-taking was in her DNA. Well, some might say this kind of relationship with her soon-to-be ex-stepfather was beyond the pale.

She couldn't care less.

She loved being near him, touching him, kissing him.

Truth be told, her real concern was Reed. How was he taking all this? Was it too early to tell?

And then there was the divorce stuff. Iz knew this was weighing down on him. Miranda wasn't making it easy on him. Big surprise.

Should she say something to her mother? Tell her to ease up. Maybe ask her what the holdup was? But if she did that, would Miranda get suspicious?

Iz sighed as she rifled through her lingerie drawer, looking for undergarments to wear for work. Some things she hadn't worn in a while. *I wonder if Reed would like me in this*, she thought, lifting a peek-a-boo pair of panties.

God, the things he did to her. She got wet just daydreaming about it. In his bed, in the kitchen, on the patio, in the pool.

And he didn't seem to mind her risk-taking side. No, he embraced it. How many adventures could they share before she had to go back to college?

School. What would happen then? Iz didn't want to think about it, but she had a gut feeling Reed might come visit her a few times, and of course, she would find time in her schedule to come home a few weekends. As long as Miranda didn't get suspicious, they could do whatever they wanted.

CHAPTER THIRTEEN

Izzy took some time on her day off to review her fall school schedule, update her Snapgram, and wash the laundry. She blasted her playlist while she texted her friends and organized her room. It was five, and shortly she'd head downstairs to start on a new Chicken Marsala recipe she found for Reed. She absolutely loved cooking for him.

Her phone rang. *Reed.* Her tummy flipped. She set down the shorts she'd been folding.

"Daddy?"

"Excuse me? This is your boss." His voice was gruff. He was playing.

Her heartbeat kicked up. "Oh, sorry, sir."

"I need to see you in my office for some dictation." He disconnected the line.

Her mouth went dry. Her fantasy. He remembered.

She silenced the music on her phone and raced to her closet. She stripped down to nothing, leaving the clothes wherever the hell they landed. She yanked a silk blouse and straight skirt off their hangers and dressed as quickly as she could. She slipped on heels, smoothed her hair with a brush, then grabbed a notepad and pen and made her way to his home office downstairs.

"Sir."

Reed looked up from his computer, dressed impeccably as usual in a pale gray suit and spa blue tie. Always the Virgo. "Please sit, Ms. Walker." He motioned to a chair he'd set up in front of his desk.

She took a seat and rested the pad on her lap; the thrill of what was to come pulsed through her veins. She was sure her peaked nipples were visible through her blouse.

"I'm looking into a new acquisition, and, well, it's a personal matter, but I have no doubt I can trust you with this information."

"Yes, sir." She wished she'd thought to wear her fake eyeglasses. It would make her look more the part.

"You can write it now and send it to me after you've typed it up. Then I'll sign it."

"Yes, sir." She could feel the adrenaline pumping. The anticipation of what he had planned was killing her.

He leaned back in his chair and began, "Dear Bruce."

That was her biological father's name.

She wrote.

"I am writing to you today—" He stopped.

She looked up at him. "Sir?"

"Ms. Walker, I mentioned this is a personal matter." He scratched his chin. "I would feel better if you would kindly move closer. Perhaps you could sit on my lap."

She swallowed and rose. Although she knew this would never happen in corporate America, for Reed, she'd always play along. "If that will help, sir."

She sat on his lap, her back to him, and laid her pad on the desk before her. His heat enveloped her.

He continued. "I am writing to you today as I wish to

make an acquisition of something you may no longer believe works well in your portfolio."

What is he talking about, she thought.

"Ms. Walker, perhaps you'd be a bit more comfortable loosening some buttons. It's after five now." He chuckled like he was making a joke and reached around to the very top button she'd intentionally closed. He undid the second and third buttons as well.

Her cheeks warmed.

"Next line. I very much prize your possession," he lowered his voice and whispered in her ear, "and believe it would be an excellent fit with me."

Moving her hair, he brushed his lips over the shell of her ear. "I would work long and hard," he emphasized the words, "to treasure your gem, show the utmost respect and pay attention to all the soft and sensitive areas that require extra special attention."

He kissed her neck, making it hard to focus. She couldn't keep up, not that she thought he'd expect her to.

"Ms. Walker, this reminds me. I've been meaning to ask you for some help with morale." He skated over her breasts, playing like it was accidental, and unfastened a few more buttons.

"Morale, sir?"

"Yes. You have gorgeous breasts. May I?" He held the lapels of her blouse and waited for her permission.

"Um, sir, I don't think HR would be okay with this."

"Oh, you know how the Big Man is," he chuckled. "'We're one big happy family here.' I don't think HR would have a problem if you share some of your assets with your boss."

He peeled away the silk, exposing her breasts.

Her heart pounded against her ribcage.

"See, these are beautiful." He cupped her breasts and gently massaged them in his big warm hands. "If the customers had more of a glance, I have no doubt our sales would skyrocket." He kissed and sucked on her neck.

"Well, sir, I already don't wear a bra."

"And I appreciate that because these are like works of art." His fondling continued and the wetness built at her pussy. "I'm thinking out loud here. Maybe there might be other things we can do to create a more energetic work environment." He caressed her breasts and pulled her back against his chest. His erection nestled into her ass. He twirled her nipples with a finger and thumb. "The image of your puckered nipples through your blouses has helped us make our sales goals last year *plus* twenty percent." He suckled her neck.

She moaned under his ministrations.

"And maybe the skirts."

"My skirts?"

He slowly yanked on the material at the side of her thighs. "Do you happen to have any shorter skirts?"

"Um, I don't know."

He hiked the skirt halfway up her thighs. "I could give you a raise, so you could buy some." He pulled the fabric higher. "Maybe this length." He pulled more, her pussy almost in view. "Hm," he muttered as if seriously considering the best course of action.

Then with a final tug, he unveiled her naked pussy. "Oh, I think this might be too short, but Ms. Walker, if I could add, you have a beautiful pussy. The aroma is breathtaking. If the office could smell like this..." He inhaled deeply.

He lifted her legs over his and spread them wide. "Ms. Walker, you are truly the best Personal Assistant I've ever had. Maybe I could show you, in some small way, how much I appreciate all you've done for me." His fingers pulled the skirt up and clear of her pussy before glossing over her thighs. "Would you like that, Ms. Walker?"

Her breasts moved up and down with her pants. She was eager for his touch, dying for his touch. "Yes, sir. Please."

"Very well." He ran his fingertips over her mound, down her lips, and up her wet slit to her swollen clit.

"Unh."

Making another pass, up and down, he avoided lingering at her needy bud. He toyed for a while, not giving her what she really needed.

"Ms. Walker, your scent is simply calling me. If it's not too much to ask, please lie your belly on my desk so I might have a little taste."

Oh, God. He was killing her. His slow, erotic commands and actions building her then making her wait. Over and over, it went. She ached to have him inside her. She loved him inside her.

"Yes, sir." She leaned forward, bent at the waist, and rested her torso on the desk with her legs spread.

He slowly pushed her skirt over her ass, leaving her completely exposed. "Such a great Personal Assistant. I love your willingness to please me." He dragged a finger over her clit, through her slit, and up to her tiny, sacred hole.

She groaned.

Using one hand, he did it again. She thought she heard fabric rustling, but when he dove in two fingers, she lost all thought. Her orgasm started to build again.

Bracing her with his large hands, he leaned down and finally laid claim to her with his tongue.

"Ah, Da— Mr. Alexander," she cried out.

His tongue ran over the same trail his finger had just created.

Incredible.

"Ah, Ms. Walker, you taste just as sweet as I thought you would." He lapped and swirled, creating pressure inside her, ready to explode with the right touch. He didn't stop.

"Oh, God," she called out as he tipped her over the edge. A glorious buildup of pleasure finally released, shooting sensation to every corner of her body and leaving her boneless.

He lifted his head, gave her a minute to calm, and spoke. "Ms. Walker, was that a satisfying experience for you?"

"Uh, yes, sir."

"Good. Maybe we should continue with the letter." With his hands on her hips, he pulled her back and lowered her down. Only his time, she was being lowered onto his cock.

She moaned long and low, letting her head fall back as she savored the contact she'd been waiting for the moment he hung up the phone.

"Oh, Ms. Walker, it appears as if you've sat on my cock. I suppose I'm okay with you being here. That is, if you are."

"Ah," she rocked slightly, "yes, sir. I am."

"Excellent." He smoothed over the insides of her thighs, not thrusting inside her, but instead letting the pressure climb slowly again. The delicious push against her walls was making her delirious with passion. Very tantric.

"Ms. Walker, your clit is very beautiful." As he circled her clit with his right hand, he brought her gently back to his left forearm. Her head lulled back. Her hair cascaded down his arm and the chair.

Arching her back with just enough lift, he raised her nipple to his mouth. "Yes," he whispered over her breast. "You do an incredible job, and now that I think of it, I would be only too happy to show you my appreciation, well, every day. If you'd like." More laving and sucking. "We could block out time on my calendar. I would be only too happy to have you straddle my lap." He made love to her breast, danced over her clit, all while tucked thoroughly inside her. It was purely maddening. "If you want, I could take you over my desk and fuck you." He sighed, still playing the game. "I suppose if you continue to show up to work without panties on, I'll know you want my cock inside of you. Yes, that would be agreeable to me."

She couldn't think. She was out of her mind with pleasure, climbing and climbing, with no sign of tipping over the edge.

She mewled as he continued his delightful torture. After several moments of the pressure climbing, she came, squirming on his lap from the tremors and his continued caresses.

"Oh, so lovely when you come. Perhaps every morning, you could come into my office. We could take a few minutes for...team building before we start our day. I know I would truly appreciate that."

He didn't stop. Instead, he lifted her head closer to his, bringing his mouth to hers to feast. He sucked in her lip and sucked on her tongue, all while her legs spread wide for him to play over her clit. His hard cock simply buried deep inside her. So deep, stretching her, she didn't know where he ended, and she began.

She pulsed her hips.

"That's right, my sweet Ms. Walker." He removed his hand from her clit and gripped her hip, holding her down, driving himself in deeper, if that were possible. "Spread those luscious legs nice and wide, arch you back, and rock over your daddy's big cock."

She shifted and rested her head on his shoulder. Then she bowed her back and pulsed her hips. Her blouse fell off her shoulders.

He brought his second hand to her hip, and as he pushed her down, he flexed his hips, gaining more space inside her.

"Ah, Daddy."

They weren't frantically fucking, no wild movements, but it was no less powerful. No less sensual and erotic.

She turned to face him, and he caught her lips. Once again

devouring her mouth. "My sexy woman. Mine. I'll come deep inside you. Come with me, baby."

She lowered a hand to rub her clit. Her rhythmic swirls and her rocking over him tipped her over the edge of oblivion.

Reed growled in her ear as he released inside, giving himself to her in so many ways.

She loved everything they shared from the role-paying, to simply talking, to love-making. Her mother was out of her mind thinking Reed wasn't enough. He gave Izzy so much. Now that he'd gotten past the idea he shouldn't be fucking her, he gave her everything she needed, and then some. Without ever questioning or judging. Iz knew she was ruined for all other men.

Chapter Fourteen

On Saturday, Reed woke the luscious woman beside him as he'd done for most of the week. He kissed and suckled her neck, her tits, and her belly. He loved how wet she got from him. And he especially loved waking up with Izzy by his side, in his bed.

He made breakfast while she got ready for work. Then they ate outside while the temperature was still mild. By noon in Dallas, the temperature could easily hit ninety.

He wrapped his arms around her, kissed her deeply, and sent her off to work. He cleaned up breakfast and the entire kitchen.

She had the lunch shift. She knew she didn't need to work —he'd told her he would give her spending money. But she'd refused. She'd said she needed to make her own money, to make a contribution.

He couldn't be more proud.

As he replayed the week, a smile tugged at his lips. For the most part, he'd made peace with having a romantic relationship with his soon-to-be ex-stepdaughter because, frankly, he couldn't be happier. He'd never felt more alive. Life seemed newer, fresher. He had more energy, and for the first time in a long time, he looked forward to every day.

She'd slept in his bed every night since Tuesday, but there was something more he could do.

While she worked her shift at the restaurant, he reorganized his bathroom and closet. There were remaining things Miranda hadn't removed; she'd taken only what she'd wanted. Reed loaded the remnants into cardboard boxes and stacked them into the garage.

It felt cathartic.

He combed the rest of the house and removed any pictures of the two of them, keeping only those of Miranda and Izzy. He also removed any tchotchkes and art he didn't like, all of which Miranda bought. Now six boxes were stacked in the corner of the garage. The last vestiges of Miranda were gone.

He walked down the hall and opened Iz's bedroom door. Her scent lingered in the air. Laundry basket in hand, he systematically moved most everything from her bathroom and closet into his. He hung her clothes, set her makeup by the second sink, and slung a fresh towel over the towel bar, right next to his. He stepped back and took it in. Temporary or not, it felt so good, so right.

Iz, Jessica, and Robert worked the lunch shift together, although Robert was doing less serving these days and more expediting. Slowly, he was working every position in the restaurant.

"Watch the balance there," Robert called as she loaded their tray with dishes for their tables.

Her eyes widened. He was right. The two lasagna plates alone could throw off her balance when she'd heft the tray to her shoulder.

"Thanks." She met his smile and rearranged her tray.

Robert took her under his wing, looking out for her, showing her the ropes—and more than just serving. Iz had the distinct feeling Robert might be interested in her. He joked more with her and smiled more than usual. He was an incredibly nice guy, funny, and cute. But wasn't it cliché for waiters and waitresses to hook up after work? She almost chuckled at herself.

She had time for dating later. She was having too much fun with Reed.

When the crowd had thinned out at the restaurant, Robert approached. "So, you have tomorrow off, right?"

"Yup. Not 'til Monday night."

"Okay, well, I'll see you in a few weeks."

Her head lifted from the saltshaker she'd been filling and furrowed her brows. "A few weeks? Why?"

"My uncle signed me up for an intensive cooking and management class in Italy for three weeks."

Her mouth gaped. "Really? That's awesome."

He grinned and nodded. "It is. And I'm really looking forward to it. They only accept twenty students for each class. Most of the time is spent at their classroom in Rome, but there are scheduled trips to Florence and Milan to several high-volume restaurants as well."

"Wow! That sounds cool."

"And I've never been to Italy, so that's exciting too."

"Well, have fun, and I guess I'll just see you when you return." It was a natural action for Iz; she turned to face him and hug him. He accepted it and even pulled her a little closer.

He held her for an extra moment, then released her. "Okay, I'm gonna check on my tables, but just wanted to tell you before you left."

"Thanks. And have fun."

He smiled and walked away.

Iz didn't bother to count her tips like the others did. Instead, she punched out, said her goodbyes, and headed for the parking lot. She couldn't wait to see Reed.

As she came through the door and walked into the kitchen, he stood over the stove, stirring something. He looked up, and his eyes sparkled at her.

"Hey, baby girl. How was work?"

She lifted onto her toes and kissed him, long and deep.

"Whoa," he said when she broke the kiss and wrapped her close.

"I missed you," she said by way of explanation.

He grinned. "I see that."

She inhaled. "Smells delish."

"We'll eat soon. Can I show you something first?" Reed held her hand and led her to his bedroom.

First, he stopped at the bathroom door threshold and motioned for her to go in. It only took an instant to see her things set up on the vanity top. Then, he opened the door beneath where he'd moved the rest of her stuff: blow dryer, curling iron, tampons, back-up shampoo, and conditioner, all of it.

She was speechless.

He guided her to the closet and pushed open the door. There on the right side were all her clothes—most hanging, some on the open shelves. He pulled open the two drawers on the right side of the dresser so she could see her bras and panties.

"Reed," she whispered. It touched her how he wanted her in his life so completely. Tears pricked the back of her eyes. "I don't know what to say."

"Do you like it?"

She stepped closer and kissed him. "I love it," she breathed over his mouth before kissing him again, more thoroughly.

There was no stopping the rush of emotion coursing

through her veins. As they kissed, her hands wandered to his shorts button and zipper. She had him free in no time.

Whether Reed intended to make love or not, he was ready for it.

God, she loved how he got hard for her. She sank to her knees and licked his tip.

"Oh fuck, Iz."

"Thank you, Daddy," were her last words before she swallowed him whole.

He growled and gripped the sides of her head.

She worked him up and down. Never before had she loved giving a man head as much as now, with Reed.

"You are so fucking good at that."

She loved his praises, but really, just loved pleasing him.

He thought about moving her things, about being closer to her, if only for the summer, and her heart soared.

He pulled back and lifted her to standing. He crashed his lips to her.

She worked free her top as he unfastened her pants. In seconds her clothes were piled on the closet floor.

In one fluid motion, he lifted her onto the dresser and dove into her eager pussy.

She moaned at the exquisite contact and wrapped her legs around him. Every time he entered her, it felt new and yet somehow like they'd been together forever.

He kissed her and gently rocked them together. "You belong in here."

"I love that you want me here and moved me into your bedroom."

"For however long you can stay, I want you here." He smiled one last time, then kissed her, consuming her mouth. His kisses trailed down her neck, and she arched, offering her breasts to him.

"Baby, you're mine." He whispered over her skin. "You belong in here with me."

She lowered her hand between them to circle over her clit. In a few short minutes, she was panting and moaning as her climax started its ascent. "Daddy—"

"Come with me, baby."

"Ah," she cried out as her orgasm ripped through her.

He growled in her ear and released with her.

She panted into his shoulder as he held her tight. His warmth surrounded her. One thing she knew as sure as the sun sets, she and Reed had a connection that neither time nor other partners would ever tear apart. A part of her would forever be his, and a part of him would forever be in her.

"I love you," she whispered into the crux of his neck.

They redressed in amicable silence, Iz pitching her uniform in the laundry basket. He smiled when she brushed her hair and applied some cream on her hands. He loved watching her in his space, making herself comfortable. He held her hand as they walked to the kitchen.

They sat outside on the patio to eat. Iz had left the white lights strung up from Memorial Day, and he knew she liked it outside.

He turned on the ceiling fan as the temperatures were climbing. He might get a bit sweaty, but he was pretty sure he could convince her to join him in a shower later. What a difference a few weeks could make.

They chatted over dinner. "So, I was thinking, next Friday or Saturday, whichever night you have off, we could go out for dinner."

The corners of her lips curved. "Okay."

"I know of a place outside of town that should be safe for us."

Her grin grew.

Of course, he could take his stepdaughter out anytime, but as a partner? That was a different thing altogether. Leaving town would give them the freedom to act like a couple without prying eyes. He could have his hands on her, kiss her whenever he wanted, and not worry who might see.

Then, he asked the question that had been on his mind for a while.

"Iz, why don't you have a boyfriend?"

She bit a bite of her home fries and shrugged. "Don't know. I had one a little while ago. He was nice enough, but it didn't work out."

"Why not?"

"We...weren't compatible. It doesn't really bother me."

He believed her. Still... He leaned in closer. "Iz, you're gorgeous, you're sweet. You could have any man you wanted."

"I have what I want."

He grinned, and she smiled back.

She lowered her fork. "Like I said, it doesn't bother me. I live my life out loud and without any regrets."

And that was the God's honest truth. Some men—boys— were intimidated by that. Iz followed her own rules. Plain and simple.

"What about you? Got your eye on someone you'd like to date?"

The thought turned his stomach. Not because it meant giving up Iz, but it meant trusting someone again.

He pursed his lips together. "I don't know, Iz."

She rested a hand over his. "Not all women are like my mother."

"I know."

"Give it some time then."

He lifted her hand to his lips and kissed it. "I'm incredibly content right now."

"Me too." She beamed. Then she glanced out at the pool and rose. "Let's skinny dip tonight."

How could he tell her no? He had a hard time denying Iz anything. And for the rest of the summer, he would take a page from her book: Live your life out loud.

Chapter Fifteen

Her period arrived. *Freakin' great timing!*

At work or not, was there ever a good time?

She retrieved a tampon and two ibuprofens from her purse in Coppola's restroom. Her tummy seemed as big as a watermelon. She dried her hands and glanced down at her phone—five o'clock. She didn't get off until ten.

The restaurant had a steady flow of customers, so Iz pasted a smile on her face. But at one point, Brenda stopped her, the sparkle in her gorgeous brown eyes dimmed.

"Are you all right?"

"I will be. Just another hour." Thankfully, by nine, the crowd was already thinning.

Somehow, she managed to make it through her shift. She texted Reed.

My cramps are horrible. Can you make me some soup?

He replied quickly.

Absolutely. I'll see you soon.

He greeted her at the door and slipped her purse off her shoulders, kissing her forehead.

"Soup's on the table," he guided her into the kitchen. "Do you need anything else?"

She inhaled the minestrone, and her tummy gurgled. "No, this is perfect. I just had some ibuprofen a little while ago."

He sat with her, sipping on white wine. When she was nearly done, he left for a moment, returning to take her hand and lead her upstairs. He was taking care of her. That was one of the things Reed did best. Her heart swelled with an appreciation for him.

She followed him into the master bedroom to hear the water running in the tub. He helped her undress, then left for a brief moment so she could take care of her needs.

She slid into the heavenly water and let the warmth envelop her.

Reed strode in and, wordlessly, leaned over the tub to caress her with a washcloth. She closed her eyes, the loving attention washing over her. After some time, he dropped the cloth and massaged her muscles, paying special attention to her shoulders, her legs, and her feet.

This man knew how to take care of a woman. How to take care of her. Iz's heart nearly burst with emotion.

Several minutes passed, and he helped her out to pat her dry. Then, he smoothed on her favorite body lotion. He reached under the vanity and handed her a fresh tampon, then retreated to the bedroom to wait for her.

"Do you want to wear pajamas tonight, baby?"

"No, that's okay." Since moving into Reed's bed, she slept naked.

Sleeping this way somehow made the connection between them stronger. As if clothes were a barrier, and now that all the barriers between them had been torn down, she would allow nothing to come between them. Certainly, it made it easy for making love. In addition to the times they weren't in bed, he'd made love to her every morning before work and every night before sleeping.

Tonight, she did wonder if she had the strength.

She slipped underneath the covers, and he joined her, naked and hard. He leaned down to kiss her sweetly on the lips.

"Reed, I don't think—"

"Shh." He pecked her again. "Making love to you isn't the only way I can show you my love."

"But you're hard."

The corner of his lip lifted. "I'm always hard when I'm around you."

He flipped off the bedside light, spooned her close, and rubbed his warm hand gently over her uterus. It felt so incredible. Her cramps began to subside, and it wasn't long before she drifted off to sleep.

He held Izzy for maybe an hour as she slept. His erection hadn't subsided, but that didn't matter. Comforting his baby girl was all that mattered. And he loved that she let him dote over her.

Reed, in some ways, felt like a new man, and it wasn't because they'd settled with the company in Taiwan. It was all because of Iz.

She'd been in his life for years, but in the past month, she'd become the center of his world. Some men might say *You lose power giving into the frivolous notions of love and romance*. But for Reed, he felt stronger. She trusted him implicitly, and he trusted her. And damn if his heart didn't slowly thaw to the idea of trusting another woman in a serious relationship again. After Miranda's betrayal, he hadn't been so sure.

And thoughts of Izzy consumed him. Even when he was talking business, he was thinking about Izzy.

Being with Iz made him feel whole. He knew it couldn't last, and in a way, he found peace with that because it meant she could find her happily-ever-after, and possibly so could he.

In the meantime, they'd share the summer together. They had two road trips coming up, more dinner dates out, and making love any chance they got. They cooked meals together, watched movies, and lounged by the pool. And it wasn't lost on him that she'd purchased more skimpy bikinis. Countless times he caught himself staring at her peacefully lying on the chaise, in her bikinis, appearing like she didn't have a care in the world.

Ah, to be young again.

She'd gotten more daring—stripping off her swimsuit to make love to him outside. If the neighbors had ventured further into their backyards, they would have seen an eyeful.

The "old" Reed would have been concerned by such brazen moves, but maybe he was loosening up because he wanted to give her what she craved, even if there was risk involved.

A smile pulled at his lips as he kissed the top of her head and drifted off into a peaceful sleep with the woman he loved wrapped in his arms.

Chapter Sixteen

Iz stripped out of her work uniform and ruminated over what to make for dinner. Her tips piled up in her bedazzled chest, resting on her vanity.

Her phone dinged with a text. Reed.

Precious.

Yes, Daddy.

I'm coming home and need to be inside you right away. I need you to play with yourself and get nice and wet. But don't come!

But you make me wet.

Uh-uh. You need to do this for your daddy. Then wait for me in the bedroom, leaning over the bed so I can get to you easily.

Yes, Daddy.

Her heart skipped a beat. First, she loved how he didn't say, "wait for me in my bedroom." She was truly in the fold of his life, at least temporarily, and that was okay. They both knew the score, and as long as it was mutually satisfying, Iz was all in.

She also loved the games they played. He would make it sound like he was her dominant, he was in control, and she was meant to serve him, but they both knew the truth. He was giving her everything she needed. Everything—the sex outside, making her masturbate for him while he watched, sneaking a feel under her skirt at dinner, or having her hands clasped behind her back while he fucked her face. It was crazy and good and nothing short of everything she wanted in a relationship. She had one month left before school started, and she would relish every single second with him.

She quickly stripped out of her clothes and lay on the bed with her legs spread. Just the thought of him coming home early to do her before dinner made her wet.

She barely got started when an idea hit her. She ran to her room to grab some nude-colored heel highs. These heels weren't really meant for walking long or far, but they were sexy as hell.

She set the shoes by the bed then lay down to warm herself up for him.

A few short minutes later, she heard the laundry room door close from the garage.

Her tummy flipped over.

She jumped out of bed, slipped on her heels, and turned to rest her hands on the mattress.

He walked in a moment later, fire in his eyes as he combed the length of her. "Looks like you followed directions."

His tie was already removed, and he slung his jacket over the back of a chair. Then, he walked behind her, a single finger glossing up her thigh, over her ass cheek, to her back. "The 'fuck me' high heels are a good choice."

"I'm glad you like them, Daddy."

"Spread those legs, baby."

She did and felt him blow a hot breath over her pussy.

"Daddy, please."

He rose, and she heard a wisp of leather through the air.

She looked to the side just as his leather belt landed on the bed. She heard the rasp of his zipper.

He leaned over her to whisper in her ear. "Baby, you know I love you, right?"

"Yes."

"I want you to say it, Iz."

"I know you love me."

He clasped her head and tilted his closer. He kissed her deeply, an all-consuming kiss. His lips were demanding and hungry, reaching into her mouth as if they were one.

The passion ratcheted her heart rate and brought another flood of liquid heat to her pussy. She ached for him, for release.

"Good. I'm going to be harder on you than ever before."

She swallowed—nervous for what was to come but excited because she knew how good her daddy fucked her.

"Head down and grab the backs of your thighs."

She laid her head down, resting on a cheek, as she reached back and clasped each thigh. She was even more open to him in this position.

"That's my girl." A deep timbre in his voice she hadn't recognized. His pants fell to the floor.

Her heart raced like a jackrabbit.

Then as quick as lightning, Reed grabbed her hair in a ponytail with one hand, another hand on her hip; he rammed into her, slamming into her end.

She screamed, partly from shock, partly from the pleasure-pain.

He thrust again, pulling her hair against the motion.

Her orgasm crashed through her before she even realized it was coming.

He pummeled her pussy over and over. Soon, a wet finger entered her ass. He pumped his finger in her ass as his cock rammed into her pussy. He added another finger, and a second glorious climax rocketed through her.

Her pussy twitched, and she trembled as the adrenaline raced through her. Her wetness slid down the inside of her thigh.

Reed was relentless, slipping in and out of her easily, yet claiming space, demanding more space inside her as if he wanted them to be one.

"God, Iz." A drop of sweat fell on her lower back.

Reed added a third finger, stretching her ass, and never breaking the rhythm of his fucking.

"You are gorgeous, baby. You are mine. All of you. Say it."

"I am...yours. All...of me." She panted, feeling another orgasm fly to the surface. She screamed out his name when it hit, feeling lightheaded at the intensity.

With her hands behind her, his fist gripping her hair, she was completely at his mercy.

Suddenly, he pulled out of her pussy and ass, only to drive his cock into her newly stretched asshole.

They both moaned.

"Ah, Iz, so tight. So beautiful... I can't wait..." He growled as he released his seed deep inside her, panting and flexing his thighs until they were flush to hers.

Soon, he grabbed her arms, wrapped them around her, and pulled her back into him. They collapsed together on the bed. Panting for several long moments, they basked in the sated, worn, and high-emotion feelings washing over them.

After a beat, he spoke. "How do you feel?" he whispered.

"Good. Sore, but good."

"You came hard."

She nodded. "Those were some of the most intense orgasms I've ever had."

He kissed her hair. "I'm glad. I won't make love to you tonight if it's too much."

She sighed. "Are you hungry?"

He chuckled. "A little. I thought we could do take-out unless you already had something going."

"I don't."

"Good. Why don't you take a bath and relax? I'll order some sushi." Then, he shifted, raised up on an elbow, and looked down on her. "Thank you, baby, for letting me fuck you. Really fuck you."

His words touched her. She loved giving him what he needed. "Miranda never let you do that." It wasn't a question.

He shook his head.

She stroked a hand along his jaw. "I love you, Daddy. My body is your body."

He kissed her, softer and sweeter than earlier. Then went to the closet to change into casual clothes.

She walked naked into the bathroom and began to fill the tub. After a few minutes, she sank in, letting the warm water soothe her body.

Her heart had grown with his every touch, his every kiss. She loved him and everything they shared. Even when he just needed to fuck her.

Early on, after he and Mom were married, Izzy could tell when he'd had a bad day and needed to blow off some steam. The house had been tense occasionally. Now she realized why. He needed to fuck, but Miranda would have no part of it. Some men stopped at the bars, or some smoked cigars or marijuana. Some were gone all weekend to golf. Reed fucked.

Then, things had shifted. Some nights, he'd come home later because he'd gone to the gym. Maybe that worked because it had never felt tense at night like that again.

Well, whatever the reason, Iz couldn't wipe the smile off her face. Maybe she liked it rough—him grabbing her hair, fucking her ass. Of course, she also knew she liked when Reed took his time, moving slowly, kissing and caressing her when they made love.

She sank a little deeper into the water. Clearly, she liked anything Reed gave her.

She wanted to give him something in return, something to show her love and appreciation. But what?

They chatted over Japanese takeout, and Iz glowed. He fucking couldn't believe how lucky he was. She would give him whatever he needed.

"Do you want to talk about what happened at work?"

She was so intuitive.

He washed down a bite of *War Su Gai* with a swallow of chardonnay. "Someone at the company broke a company policy that could put us in hot water."

He knew it was vague, but he didn't know how much detail he should tell her.

She nodded slowly. "That someone was an executive."

He nodded.

"That should have known better."

He smiled at how bright she was. "Correct."

"Was it sexual harassment?" She took a bite of her California roll.

"No, it was more along the lines of a diversity issue." The asshole manager thought he could make raises or promotions in his department to people he "liked" the most. People who looked like him. Just the thought made Reed's blood pressure skyrocket.

He'd almost gotten into a screaming match with the asshole.

They're 'employed at will'. If they don't like it, they can leave.

It doesn't work that way, he'd damn-near yelled at the guy.

He was pissed at the exec but also mad that this was happening in his company. He thought everyone *knew* better.

After a long silence, Iz set down her chopsticks and rested a hand on his. "Reed, if you have a racist bigot working for you, he's a liability, and he needs to go."

Reed almost choked on his meal at her frankness. But how right she was.

He held her gaze. He would mitigate the damage to the extent he could, probably settle for a crap-ton of money, which Cassandra deserved, to keep it out of court. Then he'd go to the execs and tell them to fire the jerk. There was no room at GS&M for that kind of behavior or attitude.

He kissed the back of her hand. "Thank you, baby. And thank you for earlier."

A broad wide smile graced her face. "Anytime."

CHAPTER SEVENTEEN

On the drive home, Reed's mind was on Iz. *What's new?* For the past several months, thoughts of her had filled his head more than usual.

He loved their connection, not just in bed but talking and daydreaming. He thought of more places he could take her, away from town, where they could enjoy the night without running into anyone they might know. He thought about a weekend getaway for just the two of them, where they could lounge around, make love, sleep in, feed each other, whatever they wanted.

He knew their special kind of relationship couldn't last, but if she wasn't dating anyone, he would love to have her anytime she came home from college.

Fuck! The sex between them was crazy good, whether making love slow and easy or like the other night when he needed a more serious release. She opened herself so willingly to him, and he wondered if he'd ever find another woman like that.

He exhaled.

But on a deeper level, Reed knew he was a changed man.

When he did get back out there, he wouldn't stop looking until he found love. Real love that reached the core.

Iz had done that. She'd cracked the shell distinctly built around his heart, wiggled her way in, and sprinkled love everywhere. Reed had never felt so free. Just like her—free to love and to be loved. Iz taught him that, and he would be eternally grateful.

He pulled into the garage, ready for a beer and a kiss from his girl. Opening the door, the smell of lasagna hit his olfactories. He turned and walked into the kitchen to see Izzy wiping down the counters, wearing a sexy French maid's outfit.

Shit!

She looked up and smiled but hadn't come over to greet him. She wanted to play.

"Oh, Isabella, I didn't realize you'd be here today."

"Yes, Mr. Reed," she said with a mock Spanish accent. "Today is cleaning day."

"Well, everything looks good." He stalked closer, pretending to survey the house.

"Thank you, Mr. Reed."

When he was close enough, she leaned all the way over the island to wipe it, causing the short skirt to hike up. He caught a lovely peek at her rounded ass cheeks. His cock came alive.

He moved behind her and casually lifted her skirt.

Fuck! She wasn't wearing panties.

"Isabella?"

"Yes, Mr. Reed."

"I see you're not wearing any underpants with your uniform. Where are your underpants?"

She stood tall, facing him. "I lost them."

He nearly grinned at the swell in her breasts. She'd worn a push-up bra just for him, not that she needed any additional enhancement.

"Lost them?"

"Yes, sir."

He let out an exaggerated sigh. "Isabella, I simply don't know what I'm going to do. I run a tight ship around here. I can't have you taking liberties when it comes to your job or your uniform."

She pulled the corners of her lips down and bowed her head, faking regret.

He crossed his arms across his chest. "How many times have we gone over this? I'm afraid I'm going to have to fire you."

"No, Mr. Reed!" She lunged toward him, gripping his shirt and plunging her breasts at him. "Please. I'll do anything. I need this job. I love my job."

He stood stock-still, feigning disappointment; his lips pursed tightly.

She lowered herself to her knees before him, her face mere inches from his crotch...and his aching boner. "Please."

He exhaled. "I suppose we could think of something you could do." He tapped a finger on his lips. "Well, since you're already on your knees, you can suck me off."

Her eyes widened. She looked from him to his bulge and back again. She reached up to work his pants, as Isabella the housekeeper would: unskilled and nervous.

All her jittering nearly had him blowing his load.

She gasped when she took him out. "Mr. Reed, oh no, you are too big for my little mouth."

"Tsk, Tsk, Isabella. I thought you wanted to keep your job."

"I do," she begged. Then, with both hands gently holding him in place, she leaned in and wrapped her lips around him.

"Fuuuck."

Her mouth was like heaven on him. She worked him up and down, fisting him at the same time.

He cupped the sides of her head and gently pushed in

deeper. Then he hit the back of her throat and nearly lost it. He flexed his muscles to stave off the climax. He didn't want this to end too quickly. His Izzy was a dream come true.

"Isabella," he said, nearly panting, "your mouth is exceptional, but I want you to stand now."

Iz rose and stood in front of him.

"It occurred to me there may be multiple infractions here. I need to inspect what else is under your dress. Please lower the top."

"Yes, Mr. Reed." Iz slowly pulled the stretchy black and white dress off each shoulder, peeling it down to her waist, leaving her chest open for his perusal.

"I see. Very good." He reached a hand to her lacy black push-up, tracing a finger along the edge. First, over the left breast, then the right, both so incredibly plump.

Her eyelids fluttered closed under his delicate treatment.

"Beautiful, Isabella. I've decided I am going to fuck you."

She gasped, fake shock taking over her expression.

He reached for a towel and handed it to her. "Lay it there," he pointed to the granite countertop she'd be wiping, "and rest your stomach on it."

She sucked in a deep breath as if she needed to fortify herself. After laying down the towel, she leaned forward, her hands folded under her cheek.

"Very good." He walked behind her, ran his fingertips up the back of her bare thighs, and slowly lifted her skirt, revealing her beautifully rounded ass. "Now, spread your legs and make room for my big cock, Isabella."

"Um, yes, sir. I don't know if you'll fit, sir."

"Isabella, let me decide that." He stroked her ass cheeks, savoring the build of her anticipation. He slid his index finger down to her precious pink pussy to check her readiness. She was incredibly wet. "Isabella, I think you're looking forward to your punishment, isn't that right?"

"Please." She begged, and he couldn't determine if it was for real or role-playing.

He lined up his cock at her entrance and pushed into her wet channel. "Fuck, Isabella, had I known your pussy was this delicious, I would have fucked you sooner."

He pulled back and drove in deeper, and she moaned.

"Lower your bra, baby, so I have something to hold on to."

She lowered her bra cups, and he reached under her, laying claim to her globes all while he continued to pump into her. He laid kisses against her bare back.

"Mr. Reed, so good. Mr. Reed." She panted. The beginning of her climax fluttered inside, tugging on his dick. He couldn't hold off anymore.

As her muscles gripped him, he released deep in her, the climax leaving him weak in the knees. He leaned over her, panting for air and kissing her back. "So wonderful, baby. I love this outfit."

"I'm so glad," she called over her shoulder.

He hated to leave but pulled out and reached for a paper napkin to wipe himself and catch what he could from her. She rose, and he lowered his head to kiss her madly. His girl knew how to make him happy, how to fill him with a love he'd never really had in his life.

He broke the kiss, taking in her flushed face. Beautiful. "I smell dinner."

She smiled. "It's in the oven. I'll be right back." She left his grasp and took three steps toward the stairs.

"Wait."

She spun around. "What is it?"

"Keep the uniform on. I may need to do another uniform inspection after dinner."

She grinned and turned back around to serve dinner for them.

Chapter Eighteen

Eight days left before Iz had to return to school. Reed had been eyeing the calendar with disgust. He was happy for her finishing up her degree but sad to not have her here with him. It would take some adjustment. Maybe he could drive there over fall break.

As Izzy got ready in the bathroom, Reed pulled a tie off the hook in his closet and laid it beside his suit jacket. He stood before the full-length mirror, buttoning his dress shirt.

The bedroom door opened.

He nearly gasped when Miranda stood in the doorway, smiling.

"Miranda." His heart leapt in his chest.

What the fuck is she doing here?

She approached him slowly. "Reed."

He recognized the tone in her voice and the sly smile on her face. She was up to something.

"Miranda, what the hell are you doing here? How did you get in?"

He glanced at the bathroom door, praying Iz wouldn't open the door.

"Some greeting. The garage." She stroked a hand down his arm like she was admiring a new shirt or something.

He schooled his face to hide the surprise and anger of her waltzing into *his* house uninvited.

She sauntered behind him meeting his gaze in the mirror. "Such a handsome man. You always were so handsome."

The tiny hairs on the back of his neck raised.

In a calm voice, he spoke again, "What are you doing here?"

She smiled. "It occurred to me that maybe we didn't talk this out properly."

Talk this out? That she wants more money? "What are you talking about?" He looped his tie, sneaking glances at the bathroom door. His heart raced.

She sat at the edge of the bed, looking up at him. "I just think there is more between us, then... Well, we can't just throw away seven good years."

What the fuck?

"And what brought this on?" It didn't matter. She needed to be gone––out of his house.

"Reed—"

"Never mind." He looked down at her, resting his hands on his hips. "We can talk about this later. I need to get to work. I have a morning meeting." That was a partial truth. He did have a morning meeting in a few hours but knowing Iz could step out of the bathroom at any second had him breaking out in a cold sweat.

Thankfully, Miranda rose. "Okay, how about we meet at Justin's after work?"

"Fine, I'll text you when I'm on my way."

She gave him a smile that once had him hopeful for the future. Now all he could think about was Iz in his bathroom and what the hell he needed to do to change the garage code.

Miranda stood at the door, stroked a hand down his chest

as if giving him a final enticement to meet her, then spun around to leave.

He closed the door and exhaled.

The bathroom door slowly, quietly opened. Iz peeked her head out.

He closed the gap between them. "She's gone."

"What the hell?"

"I know. She wants to talk. I think she wants to get back together."

Iz shook her wet head.

Suddenly the bedroom door opened.

"Reed, I went to peek in on Iz—" Miranda's words ceased as she took in the scene before her.

Iz stood fresh from the shower, wrapped in only a white towel, with Reed holding her close.

Reed stepped back and dropped his hands.

Miranda furrowed her brow for a split second, then her jaw dropped. Her eyes moved from him to Iz and back again. "I thought I'd peek in on my girl but imagine my surprise when the bed is made and empty. At eight-thirty in the morning." She stepped farther into the room. "And imagine my surprise when I see this. How long has this been going on?" Her finger pointed between the two of them.

A bead of sweat trickled down the back of his neck.

"Oh, Miranda, don't read into it." He protested.

"Ha! I don't need to. The book is wide open in front of me." She crossed her arms in front of her chest. "Reed, what the hell are you doing?"

He moved in front of the mirror again, trying to focus on his tie and appearing to not give one shit about Miranda. "Miranda, it's none of your business."

"The hell it isn't." She looked between the two of them again. "What are you doing taking advantage of an impressionable young woman?"

"Mom—"

"Don't, Iz." Miranda looked back at Reed. "My lawyer will hear about this."

"Oh, so no drinks at Justin's?" The sarcasm dripped from his voice, but inside he was quaking. She could make his life miserable.

She stepped in front of him, blocking his view, and pointed at his chest. "You'll regret this. You're her stepfather, for Chrissake."

"It should be 'was her stepfather', except my soon-to-be ex-wife keeps dragging her heels. Did you really think you could just waltz in here like this? If you can't get more money, it's me you supposedly want back." He threw his hand in the air and swiped his suit jacket from the bed. "Thanks for ruining my morning. Let me escort you out."

"We are not through." She yanked her arm free from his grip. "You'll regret this little stunt. How dare you take advantage of my daughter like that?"

She stomped off down the stairs, and after the door slammed, he spun around to see Iz standing in the same place, her mouth gaping.

He was paralyzed with fear. He couldn't move to comfort her. Hell, he could barely breathe.

"I have to go to work." It was a cowardly move, and he knew it.

Miranda's words rang in his head. She wasn't wrong. He'd taken advantage, and being the adult, he should have known better.

Jacket in hand, he turned toward the door and left.

Iz sank to the floor where she stood and sobbed. What the hell just happened? Her mother found out she and Reed were sleeping together. This was the worst possible outcome for them. Correction, Reed pulling away from her made it ten times worse.

She bawled in her hands for some time. She didn't know how long.

Please make him see we don't have to pay attention to Miranda. I'm an adult and can make my own decisions about whomever I want to have a relationship with.

Finally, she pulled herself together. Work awaited, and as much as she dreaded it, staying home crying wasn't an option either.

She finished getting dressed and went through the motions of doing her hair and makeup. Forty minutes later, she was at the restaurant. Everyone was setting up for the lunch shift. She smiled when warranted but mostly kept her head down. She worked her tables, and no one seemed to notice her world had crashed around her that morning. Several times, she'd checked her phone to see if Reed had called or texted.

She had to know everything was going to be okay between them. Of course, she cared about her mother's thoughts too, but sometimes Miranda blew things up way worse than they truly were.

Iz's stomach had twisted into knots from the minute she heard her mother's voice in the bedroom. She'd frozen in place, trying to listen to their conversation.

In time, for Iz, Miranda would forgive and forget about what she saw that morning. For Reed, she would hang this over his head. And what did this really mean for the divorce? This all started *after* Miranda had filed for divorce and moved out. But did Iz just make things worse for Reed?

God, what did she do?

As she added a ticket to the receipt bin, Robert approached her. "Let's take a break," he said.

She faked a smile and nodded.

Although Robert wasn't directly her boss, Mr. Coppola was giving him more responsibility, so Iz knew she could do what he said and not get in trouble.

Truly, she didn't want to talk. She hoped this would be short so she could finish her shift and head home. God willing, Reed would be home for dinner so they could talk about what happened.

Robert grabbed two iced teas from the drink station and followed her to the breakroom.

She sat at the round table. Emotional exhaustion was taking a toll on her.

Robert watched her drink, then asked, "Iz, what's wrong? I can see something's not right."

She dropped her head. Just hearing him ask brought tears to her eyes.

He leaned down to look at her face when a tear fell to the table. "Oh, God, Iz." He stood and instantly pulled her into his arms.

The flood gates opened, and she sobbed.

Robert was the closest thing to a friend right then, and God knew she needed a friend. His arms snaked around her, and he held her through her sobs. She had no idea if anyone had seen them as her face was buried in his chest.

This was probably the worst day of her life, but she had to believe it all wasn't supposed to end this way.

She started to calm down and lifted her head. "I'm sorry." She looked at the wetness she left on his shirt. "I'm sorry about your shirt."

"Don't worry about that. Do you want to talk about it?" His voice was gentle and sincere. Somehow, she felt like she could trust him, but no, it wasn't worth the risk.

She shook her head.

He rubbed her arms and sat her back down on the chair. He sat next to her, holding her hand. "Do you want to go home? I know you're almost done for the summer, but do you need some time off? We can all cover your shifts."

She shook her head. Working kept her busy, and at least she wouldn't be at home sulking. "No, I'm sorry. I'll be better tomorrow."

"I don't think anyone noticed, Iz. I noticed because I notice almost everything about you."

She lifted her head and met his gaze. Her tears were drying up as his words flowed through her. "You do?"

He paused a moment and nodded. "I hope that doesn't make you uncomfortable."

She pressed her lips together. She was intrigued, not uncomfortable. "No. But..." Did this mean he liked her?

He was smart, funny, and cute, but she never allowed herself to think about anything beyond "co-worker."

He cupped her other hand in his. "I find you fascinating. It's like you live your life out loud and have a million stories to tell."

She smirked. *If he only knew.*

"I don't know what's going on right now, but I hope it gets better. Truly." He looked down, then back in her eyes. "This may not be the right time, but I'd like to date you someday, Iz, and I hope that doesn't make you uncomfortable."

She fell speechless. Those had to be some of the nicest, most sincere words she'd ever heard.

"Someday. I do mean someday."

"I get that, and thank you, Robert. Thanks for everything." She leaned closer, and he met her for a hug. They embraced again and it was just the comforting she needed.

Having Robert close gave her the hope that things would work out for the best. Iz had to believe that.

CHAPTER NINETEEN

Reed sat at the bar, sipping his second glass of whiskey. He knew he should go home, be with Iz, but he was too busy sulking, too busy beating himself up to think of doing anything other than wallowing in the sorrow.

Fuck! What gave Miranda the right to stroll into his house uninvited and ruin his life? He needed to get this divorce over with, but how bad could she make it for him now?

Reed hadn't called his attorney, and at noon Phillip had called him. Reed had let it roll to voicemail. Phillip likely knew all the sorted details now, and Reed could deny nothing.

This was all his fault. What happened that morning didn't need to happen. He should have controlled the situation better. This relationship with Iz should have never started.

He slammed back the last of his drink. It tasted like battery acid, but still, he motioned to the bartender for another. At this point, he'd need to call a taxi, but he didn't care. He would sit there as long as it took to come up with a solution. Or forget the problem.

The bartender set down his drink. Reed pulled out his

phone and punched in Phillip's contact, resting his elbows on the bar top.

"Reed, I'm glad you called."

"Sorry. Am I calling too late?"

"No. As you probably know, I heard from Miranda's lawyer. He told him everything."

"Oh, I'm sure he did. Or she did. Whatever. I fucked up, Phillip. There's no sense trying to cover it up."

There was a moment of pause on the line. "Reed, I hear some background noise. Are you at a bar?"

"Yes. I needed a drink or three."

Phillip sighed. "I believe it. Listen, I'll handle things on this end. Try not to worry."

"Phillip, I need this damn woman out of my life. Whatever she wants, give it to her, just get her out." He scrubbed a hand over his face.

"I understand. Take it easy, Reed. How about you finish your drink, get a ride home, and sleep it off? Maybe take a day off tomorrow. This stress is gonna kill you."

He smirked, the closest he'd come to a laugh all day. "I will. Thanks."

Phillip disconnected.

Reed had no choice; he had to trust his lawyer. In the meantime, he had a loving, caring, likely broken-hearted woman at home he needed to consider. He knew he should steer clear of Izzy. Even just thinking it, his head dropped.

The weight of the world had never felt heavier.

Until he had a plan, he needed to avoid his precious baby girl––for both their sakes.

He was miserable. She was miserable.

A week had passed since the Miranda Explosion, that's

what Reed termed it, and he still had made no clear decision about how to proceed with Izzy.

He'd texted her a few days prior, stating he'd be working late and that he wanted to take some time to figure out the next move for the sake of everyone.

She'd replied that she missed him and wished they could work it out together.

If only it were that easy.

Miranda had called him the day before, but he let it roll to voicemail. He shouldn't have listened to her message, but he did:

I am still shocked at how cavalier you are with our daughter. She is young and impressionable. I expected more from you, Reed. I just want to know how long this has been going on. And how dare you get mad at me for my tiny indiscretion when you are having sex with Izzy. I am simply at a loss for words.

Well, apparently, she hadn't *really* been at a loss for words because after several minutes, her voicemail had stopped recording and disconnected the line.

He dragged himself out of his empty bed and went through the motions of getting ready for work.

He stared at the coffee maker, waiting for his cup to fill. Breakfast didn't appeal to him, but he grabbed an apple from the crisper drawer. He'd lost his appetite and consequently lost weight. His memory wasn't as sharp either. He knew all the stress was eating at him.

He needed to figure this shit out soon.

Grabbing his apple and travel mug, he headed for the garage. He made it to the car when he realized he'd forgotten his laptop. He left the coffee and apple and turned back to the house.

Lifting his laptop case from the barstool, he froze.

He couldn't be sure, but he heard something that sounded like crying. Izzy crying.

What the hell?

Another minute passed. it *was* Izzy. He had to do something. This couldn't fucking continue.

In some respects, he was weak around Iz, and in some, he was strong. At that moment, he chose strong.

Who knows how many tears she'd shed over this whole fiasco? Miranda had found out. Nothing could be done about that, but he knew Iz was heartbroken, and so was he. Well, all this shit needed to end. To hell with Miranda.

He took the steps two at a time and made it to Izzy's bedroom door. He opened the door to see her wiping her eyes with a tissue and hugging a teddy bear close.

"Iz."

She gasped and looked his way. "Reed."

He went to her and sat on the side of the bed.

She shifted and wiped away the tears, but the miserable look couldn't be wiped away.

He grabbed her hands. "Iz, I'm so sorry this happened." He kissed her lips because he couldn't think of another way to give her some comfort right then. "I'm sorry I let this happen."

"It's not your fault, Reed."

"It is, but guess what, I don't care about Miranda. Well, I don't care what she thinks." He pecked her lips again.

Her eyebrows rose. "You don't."

"No. Have you spoken to her?"

"Yes, briefly. I told her I'm old enough to make my own decisions."

"You are."

"Well, she still thinks I'm five, I guess. She said she was disappointed in you. I told her that I wanted this, but she wouldn't hear of it."

A small smile pulled at his lips, hearing her defend him to her mother. He cupped her jaw and drew her in close for a deep kiss. A kiss to tell her just how much she meant to him.

"Thank you, baby."

She moved closer to him, pressing her body against his to return the kiss. "I missed you. I know this won't be easy, but we can get through this together," she whispered over his lips.

"Yes, we can." He circled his arms tightly around his baby girl, then pulled her onto his lap. He needed to feel her warm body against his, showing him, she was real. That she'd never left.

Straddling him, she pushed off his jacket, then his tie, and started working on his shirt buttons. Her hands roamed his exposed chest as she resumed her all-consuming kisses.

"Daddy," she breathed over his mouth.

"Whatever you want, baby girl. I'm not going anywhere."

Her eyes sparkled now with joy, not tears. She pulled off his shirt and tossed it aside.

He pulled her T-shirt over her head, giving him beautiful access to her warm, generous body. She was his precious baby, and he would give her the moon and the stars. He cupped, massaged, and loved on her breasts with his mouth.

In her eagerness, she worked his pants free. Reaching in, her hand wrapped around his hard cock. She stroked him a few times before shimmying closer. She pulled her thong aside and sank down onto him.

They both moaned loudly.

"I love you," he whispered over and over on her lips, her neck, and her breasts.

"Daddy," she groaned. She rocked over him, working her way to ecstasy.

He sucked hard on a nipple and sent her over the edge.

She cried out his name.

He kissed her one last time, then spun her around to lie on the bed and pulled out.

Her panties came off in an easy tug. Next, he shoved at his

pants and briefs, yanked off his shoes and socks, and covered her sweet body with his.

"I love you," she whispered over his lips before she pulled him down to her warm, waiting mouth. Her tongue danced with his.

He could feel the desperation in her kiss because he had it too. The last week without Iz was brutal.

She was right; she was old enough to make her own decisions. Whatever it took, they would convince Miranda that she didn't have a fight. They would be together if they wanted for as long as they wanted.

Reed slipped back inside his love, and she bowed off the bed, panting as she moaned his name. He made love to her for an hour. Even as he came, he never left his love.

They shared a bond that nothing could break. He just needed to be reminded of that.

He kissed her entire body, and then she pushed him on his back to love on him.

They whispered professions of love and desire. Of how fulfilled they both felt. And regardless of how long it'd last—which they would decide when it would end—this summer was the happiest, most amazing summer they ever had. They made a pact to always be in each other's lives.

As they shared one final climax together, Reed held her close, both of them panting to recover their breaths. Slowly, he turned them on their sides, and they stared for several long moments, savoring the togetherness.

He was a fool to listen to Miranda and abandon Izzy. She was the light of his life and always would be.

His phone chimed with a text. That might be the first text of the day or the hundredth. He was too engrossed in sharing this precious time with Izzy to be bothered to pay attention to his damn cellphone in his jacket pocket.

"How about I take the day off?" He pecked her nose with a kiss.

Her whole face lit up. "Yea? That would be wonderful."

He rummaged for his phone to text Nikia and ask her to reschedule his meetings. He saw the cause of the text notification: Phillip.

Got everything squared away. Sending a final contract to your office to sign. You'll like it.

His smile spread, and he met Iz's gaze.

"What is it?" Iz asked as her perfect eyebrows pulled together.

"Looks like I'm about to be free and clear. We're gonna celebrate tonight. But first..."

He flipped her around to all fours and easily entered her.

Iz moaned long and low. Pure music to his ears.

CHAPTER TWENTY

Izzy had asked him to take her to work on her last day and to pick her up that night. It seemed she was interested in a coworker and wanted him to meet the boy. Reed was happy for her. Ultimately finding somebody her own age would be key in the success of her romantic life.

Frankly, Reed wanted to see this nephew, Robert, for himself. The boy who seemed to take an interest in *his* girl.

His current relationship with Iz might be temporary, but he would never stop looking over her, as a father would. If this boy was no good for her, Reed needed to know it right away.

He turned off the car and stood, leaning against the driver's door in Coppola's parking lot.

After a few short minutes, he noticed the last of the lights in the restaurant go out.

The boy, Robert, walked alongside Izzy as they headed in Reed's direction. He wore his black and white uniform and stood an inch or two shorter than Reed. The only other car in the parking lot was a black, mid-priced sedan.

Good, a nice safe car.

Iz approached him. "Daddy," she rarely called him that in public, "this is Robert. Robert, this is Reed."

"Good to meet you, Mr. Alexander." The boy had a sincere smile and a strong handshake.

"You too, Robert. I understand your uncle owns the restaurant."

"That's right. It's been in the family for a while. My cousin is working on his doctorate and has no interest in running a restaurant, so one day my uncle wants me to take it over."

"Nice. Will you be able to go to college too or is that not possible?"

"Well, I graduated already with an econ degree. I don't know how much I'll use it in the restaurant business, but that's okay." He grinned. "I love working here. And I love the idea of running my own business."

Reed admired the kid's drive. "I see. And perhaps someday you'd also like to date Iz?"

Robert met his inquisition easily. "Yes, sir. If that's all right with you."

He glanced down at Iz, standing beside him, and casually snaked an arm around her waist. "What do you say, baby? Would you like to go out with Robert sometime?" That was the real question. This wasn't the fifties when a father's approval had been required.

She lifted up to peck his lips. "Yes, Daddy," she said loud enough for the boy to hear. With a hand cupped around the back of his neck, she guided him for another kiss, this time diving in deep, devastating his mouth.

Whoa!

Reed returned the kiss and wrapped a hand around her upper back.

Her hand slid south and cupped his ass cheek.

His dick came alive in an instant.

When she finally pulled back, he let her go.

Robert stared, his expression unreadable. *Impressive.*

She stepped toward Robert, smiled, and pulled a piece of paper from her apron pocket. "Here's my cell phone. Call anytime." She stepped close, leaned up, and placed a lingering kiss over his lips.

Reed knew that kiss. The power in the kiss drew a man in.

Fuck! She knew just what she was doing.

She smiled at him one last time and spun around to head to the opposite side of the car. "See you over Thanksgiving break."

Reed smiled and opened his car door. He started the car and, with one last look at the boy, he saw the gentle smile tugging at his lips.

He might be a boy in Reed's eyes, but he was full of understanding.

"You little vixen," Reed said as they pulled onto the street.

She leaned over to kiss his cheek and neck and cup his erection. "Daddy, I'm not ready to give you up yet."

"I see that. And you want it all, huh?" His words came out with extreme concentration as her hand did wonderful things to him.

"I do. Do you blame me?" she whispered.

He chuckled. "No."

"Please, Daddy. Please take me somewhere and fuck me now." Her words floated by his ear, then she began loosening his jeans.

He drove the short distance away from the congested area to a quiet, dead-end alley. A large office building stood to their left, completely vacant at this hour, and two small, older buildings on the right, also empty.

She reached for her button and zipper and slid off her pants, then worked free her top.

His cock thickened, and desire flowed through his veins. He pushed against his jeans to make her room.

She swung a leg over him and sunk down on him instantly.

"Fuck, Iz."

She fit him like a glove.

"You're not ready to give me up either," she murmured as she trailed kisses over his cheeks and neck.

Fuck no, but it's inevitable. "I love you. You know that," he whispered before ravishing her lips.

She moaned into his mouth.

He pulled back. "At some point, I will need to set you free."

She rocked over him, her back arching through the movement.

He pulled her bra cups off her breasts for him to feast.

"Unh. I know, Daddy," she panted, "but I'm not even ready to get married yet. I'm too young."

"But date, Iz. That's how you find your future husband," he stated the obvious. "Give Robert a chance."

"Daddy, I will. You feel so good. This is what I want too."

Reed put it together in an instant. "Will you fuck him while you're also fucking me?"

"Of course." She gasped before her orgasm crashed through her.

He smirked. He should be surprised, but he wasn't. "You little vixen."

THANK YOU!

Thank you so much for reading Virgo!
Make sure you check out the next book in the series, Scorpio!

If you enjoyed this story, please consider posting a review at one or more of your favorite retailers, as well as Goodreads. Even a short review, one or two lines, can be a tremendous help and encouragement to the authors. Your review is also a gift to other readers who may be searching for just this sort of story, and will be grateful you helped them find it.

Thank you!

Bonus: for a deleted scene from Virgo, click here: https:// BookHip.com/XGSQVSK

Excerpt from Scorpio

Chapter One

Scarlett tugged at the short skirt of her dress, wishing she'd worn something longer.

Was it always this short? Maybe it shrank or maybe I gained weight, she thought as she sipped her margarita.

Glass was packed that night. Partiers came out en masse to dance, drink, and watch the live band.

Scarlett, Shayla, Rose, and Tinker came out to celebrate Tinker's thirtieth birthday.

Shay called out. "Selfie. Get close."

The women smiled as everyone clicked their camera one at a time. Scarlett's attention was momentarily pulled away when a group approached the bar. Mostly couples from what Scarlett could see, but that didn't stop her eye from being drawn to one tall hottie with the best fitting jeans she'd ever seen on a man.

She swallowed and turned her attention back to her girls.

When Bruno Mars came on, Tinker jumped up. "Woo hoo. My song. Let's go."

Scarlett smiled. Just about every song was *my song* to Tinker.

Tinker was the music buff. Rose was the movie buff. Seemed like every movie was her "all-time favorite". Shayla was the health and nutrition nut. Scarlett, well, she was the hopeless romantic. Anything and everything from romance books and toys to Valentine's Day and hot dates. Her mind constantly raced with ideas for dates, positions, poems. Shay would tell her it's because she was a Scorpio and her keyword was sex.

That'd made Scarlett laugh out loud. She'd had a total of four boyfriends.

As the girls danced, some men would join in for a dance or two. By the fourth song, Scarlett was ready to sit, but lookie there! Mister Nice Jeans showed up on the dancefloor.

His arm muscles told her he had a very intense job or he was a gym rat. Which might explain the incredible way his jeans fit him. His dark brown hair had a gentle wave to it that Scarlett imagined would be great running fingers through. Her fingers.

Oh. He had a dance partner.

Scarlett sighed inside. Why was it all the good-looking ones were taken?

His gaze caught hers, and she almost froze. He had the most incredible gray-blue eyes. Maybe it was the colored lights; she'd never seen a color like that on a person.

Scarlett couldn't look away. Her breathing came shallow. His gaze drew her in.

Then, the girlfriend with her long blonde hair, her eye-popping lush boobs, and her perfect tight butt said something and pulled his attention.

Scarlett looked toward the bathrooms in need of some space. "Be right back," she called to her girls.

They nodded.

Scarlett leaned against the vanity countertop, a flush evident in her cheeks. She wetted a napkin and patted her face, then reapplied her lip gloss. She didn't know what came over her. He was just a guy. She couldn't think, couldn't move, and couldn't breathe.

It was some kind of weird, cosmic reaction that would be best forgotten.

She slung her tiny purse across her body, pulled down her dress, and made her way out to the chaos.

She stopped at the bar for a fresh drink, deciding to hang back at the table for the next few dances.

"What can I get ya'?" the bartender leaned forward.

"A Truly, please."

"Hi." Mister Nice Jeans strode up beside her.

When Ryan first locked eyes with the beauty across the bar, he had to make some contact with those penetrating eyes. He felt drawn to her, might she feel the same? He'd watched her head to the bar and thought this was his chance.

She looked over. "Hi."

"I've never tried those. I guess they're pretty good." The lame opening line made him cringe inside.

"They are." Her smile and eyes were captivating.

The bartender set down her drink with a napkin. As she reached into her purse, Ryan had his credit card ready. "Two more of those, all on this, please." And handed the card to the bartender.

"Thank you." She gazed up at him.

He smiled. "You're welcome." He offered his hand. "Ryan McManus."

She clasped it. "Scarlett Jones."

He repeated her name in his head and he liked the sound of it.

He lingered a bit too long and broke their handshake. If Janis looked over at that point, it would be awkward.

As much as he hated to leave, he lifted his drinks and said, "Well, nice to meet you Scarlett Jones."

"You too. And thanks again for the drink."

He raised a can and smiled as he walked away.

The inexplicable warmth crept over Ryan. No matter how brief it was, he went out of his way to meet Scarlett.

He handed the Truly to Janis. "Here ya' go. I thought we'd try something new."

"Oh, Ryan, I don't know if I'm gonna like this." She wrinkled her perfect nose.

"If you don't, I'll go get you an Old Fashioned." He should have known not to try and surprise Janis. She hated surprises.

As the group waited for the band to start, Ryan stole a few glances at Scarlett from across the room. He watched her dance and laugh. Her eyes sparkled when she smiled.

Derek leaned close, snapping him out of his gaze. "The guys wanna head to Benny's."

"We haven't even been here an hour." Ryan wasn't ready to leave.

Derek shrugged a shoulder. "They don't like the band."

He stole one last glance at Scarlett, and they headed out. It was great while it lasted.

Chapter Two

If there was ever the dreaded Monday, this was it.

Scarlett dragged her ass into her apartment and kicked the door closed behind her. She plopped her bags on the table, then looped her purse on the back of a kitchen chair and started rifling through the few groceries she'd purchased. After reaching for the open bottle of white wine on the fridge door, she poured herself a glass.

This was what she needed to forget work awhile.

Before she could take her third sip, Shayla strolled in.

"Hey, chica. How's it going?"

"Long day. A typical Monday."

Shay grimaced. "Pour me one of those, and I'll be right back." She strode down the hall toward her bedroom.

Scarlett poured her a glass and sank into a chair. After a few short minutes, her roommate took the seat next to her at the kitchen table, clinked her glass, and said, "Cheers."

"I bought chicken for dinner."

Shay nodded. "Great. Now, wanna talk about your day?"

Scarlett let out a sigh then filled Shayla in on her crazy and exhausting day. Handling a portion of the online marketing for the largest orthodontia practice in Texas put a lot of responsibility on her shoulders. She had come up with an advertising campaign for Amarillo, doing the best she could with the limited info on the brief sent in from the field rep.

A brief was a request of what the field offices needed to run a marketing promotion. Her proposal got kicked back with a nasty note stating it was all wrong. *And* the rep had copied her boss.

"So, go back, clarify the brief, and give these guys what they're looking for. If anyone can turn out a gorgeous product, you can." Shay always had a straightforward and simplified way of seeing things.

Scarlett grinned and saluted her with her wineglass.

Over less serious conversation, the two made dinner and within twenty minutes were sitting together and eating a nutritious, low-carb dinner.

"When does Dave come back?"

Dave was Shayla's boyfriend for the last six months. He'd left the night before for a business trip to Chicago. He did accounting with First Financial and rarely needed to travel, and Shay missed him already.

"Thursday." She glanced at her phone. "He's doing the group dinner thing, so I'll call him later."

"Good. Wanna watch a movie tonight?" Scarlett could use a good distraction, have some laughs, crash in bed, and get ready to do it all again the next day.

Shay rose from the table, taking the empty plates to the sink. "I have a better idea. You've had a rough day. Let me get my table, and I'll give you a massage."

Scarlett wanted to do backflips. "Really?"

"Yes, really. All you have to do is ask," her friend insisted.

"I know, Shay, but I feel like I'm imposing since this is your job. Fifty plus hours a week."

"Oh, please. Strip," she commanded as she walked out of sight in search of her portable massage table.

Scarlett knew not to argue. She stripped out of her clothes as Shay set up her table. Then she laid face down. "Thanks again." She was too tired to feel guilty; she needed this massage in the worst way. She knew she'd feel a million times better afterward.

Shayla covered her with a blanket before she turned on music on her smartphone and dropped it into the speaker. She flipped off the lights. Scarlett heard the top pop on the lotion and felt Shay's hands caress her neck and shoulders.

"Try not to think about work." Shay made several passes

down her back and out over her shoulders. "Think about that hottie from Glass."

"Ryan."

"Yeah. Think about him."

"Uh, that could be dangerous," she said with a smile. "It's been eight months since I've been with a man." She feigned an exasperated tone.

Shay snickered.

"Where are you tight the most? The usual?"

"Yes, plus I'm horny."

Shayla belted out a laugh, and Scarlett joined in.

Shayla swatted her behind. "Stop making me laugh. I can't concentrate."

"Yes, ma'am."

Most of the massage continued in silence. There was the occasional comment or question, or the involuntary groan slipping passed Scarlett's lips. The massage was all she could have asked for. Plus, Shay gave special attention to her glutes and hips.

Shay was the best in her field. She would implement different techniques based on what the muscles felt like. With years of experience, she had a clientele list a mile long. She loved her job, and it showed.

Every once in a while, she'd hit a tough spot. "Take a deep breath and blow it out."

Scarlett grimaced when Shay worked on a knot.

"Pretend I'm Ryan giving you a massage."

She smiled. "I can do that."

"He was fine. Handsome face, nice muscular body, and a smile that could cream your panties."

Scarlett chuckled. "He *was* hot. Too bad he had a girlfriend."

"Seriously."

"Okay, flip."

Scarlett rolled over, and Shay repositioned her blanket and started on her arms and pecs.

After some time, Shay continued working her magic up and down her legs, hips, and feet. Interestingly enough, the suggestion about a hot man doing this to Scarlett's awaken her lady parts. Her nipples peaked, and her breathing changed.

Shay must have noticed because she asked, in that caring way she had, "How ya' feelin'?"

"Fine."

"You seem a little turned on right now."

She smirked. "I guess." Scarlett knew she was if the ache at her sex was any indication.

A small pause. "Hm. Do you want me to give you an orgasm, babe?"

OTHER BOOKS BY MIA LONDON

Kaleidoscope Series:

Black Tie

Blue-Eyed Devil

Firecracker Red

Angel In White

The Yellow House Next Door

Pretty in Purple

A Smattering of Gray

Plush Pink Lips

Lush Lavender (*coming soon*)

Scarlet Silk (*coming soon*)

Second Chance at Love (Chance at Love, 1)

Only Chance at Love (Chance at Love, 2)

Honeymoon Hideaway

Runaway (Cascade Mountain Manhunt, 1)

Renegade (Cascade Mountain Manhunt, 2)

Accidental Tryst

Perfect Seduction (Perfect, 1)

Perfect Surrender (Perfect, 2)

Beyond Lace (Hard Men of the Rockies, 4)

Undeniable Fate (Undeniable, 1)

Undeniable Love (Undeniable, 2)

Dry Spell (Sweet Escape, 1)

Hot Spell (Sweet Escape, 2)

Cold Spell (Sweet Escape, 3)

Life To The Max

Wanton Angel, Prequel to Life To The Max

Zodiac Heat

Virgo (Zodiac Heat Book 1)

Scorpio (Zodiac Heat Book 2)

About the Author

Mia London loves to write.

After reading fiction for years, she decided it was finally time to put those images and scenes floating around in her head down on paper.

She is a huge fan of romance, highly optimistic, and wildly faithful to the HEA (happily ever after). Her goal is to create a fantasy you will enjoy with characters you could love.

She lives in Texas with her attentive, loving, super-model husband, and perfectly behaved, brilliant children. Her produce never wilts, there are no weeds in her flowerbeds and chocolate is her favorite food group.

Email: mia@mialondon.com

You can find Mia on the following Social sites:

Facebook.com/MiaLondonAuthor

Twitter.com/mialondonauthor

Instagram.com/mialondonauthor

Goodreads

Bookbub

YouTube

www.ingramcontent.com/pod-product-compliance
Lightning Source LLC
Chambersburg PA
CBHW061453210726
48287CB00007B/2490